"ALL THE WORLD'S A STAGE,
AND ALL THE MEN AND WOMEN MERELY PLAYERS;
THEY HAVE THEIR EXITS AND THEIR ENTRANCES..."

—WILLIAM SHAKESPEARE, AS YOU LIKE IT

Prologue

"Ugh... Fuck...," I groaned, *watching* the leaves fall and tumble outside the window.

"C'mon, don't be such a puss, Owen. I know this ain't your first," Serena chuckled. She pulled the needle away from the skin over my ribs, ensuring I wouldn't end up with crooked lines, and eyed me, eyebrow raised.

"This *ain't* my first, but it might just be my last," I replied, my voice oozing with sarcasm. We both knew I couldn't possibly be serious. It was an addiction. One I absolutely loved to maintain.

"Then grind your teeth and shut your cakehole. I don't like wussy clients."

She sounded like she meant business, so I tried to remain quiet.

I couldn't even tell you why it hurt so much. She was right. It wasn't my first tattoo, yet it was the first one that truly felt uncomfortable. Painful, even. I didn't know if it was because of its placement or its design, although I am sure anyone who asked about its meaning could draw their own conclusions. I wouldn't be able to disagree, either. It was meant to cover up a scar not visible to the naked eye. A scar that came with a constant ache. An ache for *her*. An ache no one could understand. However, to me, it was more real than anything, especially this time of year. Fall had been when she arrived, and with each falling leaf, I missed her more.

"All right, lamo. You're done."

Serena smiled, scooting her chair back and setting the machine down before grabbing her spray bottle and a few paper towels. After wiping my ribs down, she motioned toward the full-length mirror on the wall, throwing away the smeared paper towels – evidence of her new piece of art.

Standing, I took a deep breath, stretching out the kinks from sitting for so long. While most yearned to see their finished ink at the end of the session, I seriously dreaded it with this one. If it wasn't perfect, it wouldn't just be a messed up piece of art. It would be a messed up... *her*. Closing my eyes for a moment, I turned slowly and faced my reflection, moving my arm just enough to see what would now grace my skin forever.

A beautiful raven, spreading its wings across the left part of my torso, its piercing green eyes located just about where my heart was.

My scar.

"It's beautiful," I said in a hoarse voice, my fingers hovering, aching to touch it, to trace the outlines.

"Hey, shithead, no touching the new art! If you get it infected, it'll be my reputation that's going down the drain. What's your fascination with ravens anyway?" Serena asked, walking over with some goo to apply, as well as some plastic wrap to turn me into a human burrito.

"If only you knew...," I mumbled quietly, watching the raven do what Rayven did best... disappear.

Chapter 1

"**W**hat's with the new ink?" Destiny asked as she rolled over, her bare nipples grazing my side when she reached out to touch my chest.

"Don't fuckin' touch it. That's what's with the new ink," I all but growled, grabbing her wrist as soon as her fingertips connected with my skin, gently but determinedly pushing her away.

"Please, you've never been opposed to this," she purred seductively, softly running her nails down my abs to where the blanket covered the lower half of my body.

"You've just had your fill – literally, I'd say," I said with a smug smirk. "Now, put your slutty little outfit back on and get off the bus so the guys can get back on. We've got a journey to make."

"Slutty little outfit?!" she asked, sounding appalled, which I knew she definitely wasn't. She liked to play. Thankfully, I had figured her out and moved beyond playing cat and mouse long ago. Knowing her ways made being around her a lot more bearable, but she had stopped being my "destiny" in our senior year of high school. Personally, I had no intention of igniting an old flame.

"Chop-chop, Dee. I got somewhere to be. Without you."

"Can't I come? You're a freaking rock star now, Owen. People won't even notice. You're always surrounded by a bunch of girls anyway. What's one more?"

"A nuisance." I climbed out of my bunk, butt naked. "And I already let you come. More than once."

"Mmm, you sure you want me to go? I, myself, am quite enjoying the view. I wouldn't mind seconds... and more." She smiled, propping herself up on her forearms in an attempt to show herself from her best side. Truthfully, though, it made her look cheaper than she was... which, seeing as she'd been free, was saying a lot. She never even cost me dinner or a drink anymore, and the quick call or text didn't count, seeing as I had a flat rate and she wouldn't even be another number on the bill.

"I'll be nice and ask you to get the fuck out one more time. If you make me ask again, it'll be Dillon getting your ass outta here... dressed or not."

Dillon was our main roadie/bouncer/bodyguard... and one hell of a scary sight. He towered over my six-foot, one-inch frame and was about twice my size with stone-hard muscle. It had occurred to me more than once that people might just think he carried the portal to faraway lands inside of him.

Maybe if I run into him with enough force...

"Owwwwennnn," she pouted, interrupting my derailing train of thought, getting up slower than a snail that had aged beyond its life expectancy.

"I'm serious, Destiny. You know the conditions of coming here. You're no more or no less to me than any other girl who sets foot on the bus and takes her clothes off for me. Just another stain on the sheets. I have made that clear from the start, so don't fucking start with me *now*."

"You've become so... cocky."

Her obvious frustration was a balm for my soul. Maybe she was right and I wasn't the person I had used to be. Losing people will do that to you, though.

I shrugged. "I'd say distant, but I'll take cocky." I pulled my black jeans on, closing the buckle of my belt without even looking at her.

"You're an ass."

"A fine piece of cocky ass you keep coming back to. Feel free to uninvite yourself from the party. I'll have no trouble finding someone else. Oh, wait... That'd take away your thirty seconds of fame, wouldn't it?"

I could feel her staring daggers into my back as I slipped on my combat boots, pushing the laces inside of them rather than taking the time to tie them.

"Thirty seconds?! Don't sell yourself short."

Rolling my eyes at her repeated attempt of flirting with me, I tossed her dress at her, which couldn't have been made of any more fabric than one designed for a five-year-old. Pulling a tank over my head and grabbing my cigarettes, I threw her a look.

"Three... Two..."

"What are you counting down to? Round two?" She smiled, at least being smart enough to slip on her heels. "Don't worry. I'm out of here. You're no fun when you're grumpy."

"I'm not grumpy. I'm just sick of you," I said with a sweet little smile of my own, which I was sure didn't reach my eyes. I opened the door of the bus and stepped outside, lighting my cigarette.

"Is Destiny not wanting to leave again?" Chuck asked amusedly, taking a swig of beer. "When are you ever going to learn?"

"Believe me, it's a matter of learning by doing, but I'm getting there."

Rolling my eyes, I inhaled a big drag, enjoying the way the smoke burned down my lungs. I'd been meaning to quit because smoking wasn't doing my vocal chords any good, but it was a nasty habit that stuck like gum to a shoe... or in hair. Whatever the saying was. Or like Destiny to me, all things considered.

"You know, I can hear you," Destiny huffed as she hopped off the bus, making sure to flaunt as much of her chest as possible without being considered undressed, which must have taken some serious effort.

"Good. It means you would've also heard if I'd called Dillon," I said with an angelic expression, wiggling my fingers in a little wave.

"Call me?"

Shit. Why did she have to sound so hopeful? Shouldn't she be sick of how I treated her? Be on the run? Block my number? Keep her legs closed? Put on a chastity belt and throw away the key?

"I'll try not to," I sighed, running a hand through my hair before taking another long drag of my cigarette, my heart pounding. I could only hope Rayven wasn't doing the same kind of walk of shame in an alternate universe right at that very same moment.

Chapter 2

"**D**uuuuuude, that was fuckin' sick! The crowd was cray-cray-craaaaaazaaay!" Jimmy chuckled as he draped his arm over my shoulders, half of his whiskey spilling over the rim of his glass and onto my shirt. Mixed with the sweat glistening on my body from rocking the stage, it was set to make a great cologne – a smell that would have the fans going more nuts than the fresh fragrance evaporating off one's body after a long, hot shower. I'd probably never come to fully understand that.

"Mhm, yeah. It was great," I agreed unenthusiastically, despite the adrenaline from performing in front of thousands still rushing through my veins. It had been a great show and would have been perfect had *she* been there.

Shaking off the feeling of melancholy, I grabbed his glass, downing the rest of the piss-warm amber liquid that had remained after the spillage.

"You're a stellar stallion, man. What's with the grim face?" he asked, handing me an almost empty bottle of bourbon. "Get your panties out of their twist! I don't wanna hear you say another word before you've gotten to the bottom of this, you sexy beast!"

"Geez, how drunk are you, Jimmy?" Cocking an eyebrow, I slowly eyed one of my best friends. He stepped away, shrugging, a twisted expression on his face – a mixture of trying to look angelically innocent and trying not to laugh, combined with bordering on the land of the wasted.

"I might've had one, or two, or four of something before and during the show... and right after... and in between," he offered as he walked away, grabbing another bottle of God-knows-what on his way toward the backstage lounge, a place that would soon look unrecognizable and as wasted as we'd soon feel. "Go and bang a smile onto that pretty little face of yours!"

Coming down from a high after a show was the worst. It was those moments in the spotlight that, while not allowing me to forget about her, at least pushed her farther into the back of my mind. It allowed me to live in the moment, the then and there, rather than the past. Once a show was over, though, she came rushing back to the forefront of my mind, infiltrating my every fiber, my every thought.

She would have absolutely loved all of this – the excitement, the music, the traveling, the songs.

"You... You don't know what music is?" I asked in disbelief, absolutely astonished. How could someone not know what music was? Unless they were deaf, but even then, they were usually still familiar with the concept. Some even had a much better feel for rhythm than people who could hear. So how could someone not hard of hearing have never even heard of music?

"I... No," she offered reluctantly, her answer sounding more like a question than anything. The way she looked at me conveyed the fact my words had apparently made her feel as if she had forgotten something substantial, something that was extremely important to remember. Or maybe it was because I looked at her as if she had grown three heads. Not like either one of those options would have been preferential...

"It's, uh... sounds." How do you explain something so normal to you? So normal, yet so extremely important.

"Sounds...," she repeated slowly, obviously thinking about it for a moment, letting it sink in. "You mean, like, singing?"

"Yes!" I nodded, a relieved smile tugging on my lips. At least she knew what singing was. "But underlined with music."

"We're kinda turning in circles." She chuckled a bit. Damn, what a beautiful sound. Ironically, I could have said it was like music to my ears.

"Well, uh, with instruments."

"In...struments?" She frowned, making it sound like two separate words, obviously still not quite sure what I was talking about.

With a frustrated sigh, I threw my hands up in defeat, wondering just how fucking hard she had been hit on the head. Maybe I had broken her brain, if that were somehow anatomically possible. I doubted it, but it wasn't like I was anywhere close to being a straight A student, and I had only ever paid attention to certain parts of Anatomy class.

"Just... Come with me. You'll see."

"Will it hurt?" she asked quietly, a cute little frown line appearing between her brows. Whether she were being frustrating or adorable was highly debatable at that very moment. Maybe she was just messing with me? Trying to see how gullible I was?

"No, not unless you want it to," I smirked. For some reason, my words brought a little color to her cheeks. Good to know where her mind was.

I led her to the garage adjacent to the house, then picked up my guitar and started strumming some chords, letting them fade into a light melody, my eyes never leaving hers. Her reaction mesmerized me, seeing her getting lost in the sound I created, discovering music for what seemed like the very first time.

After a while, she cleared her throat and averted her eyes. That was my cue to stop, so I picked at a few more strings before slowly removing my strumming hand from my guitar. Almost immediately, her eyes snapped back to mine, meeting an inquisitive look.

"So... What do you think?" I asked softly, hating that one thought or another must have pulled her out of her reverie, out of the almost intimate moment we had shared.

Looking at me in silence, which made me more nervous than it should have, considering we had only met mere hours before, a small smile spread slowly across her features.

"It's like... the sound of feelings," she breathed out, absolutely in awe of the melody that had radiated from the instrument in my hands.

"So you liked it?" I asked, surprised at how insecure waiting for her answer made me. Since when had I, Owen Connors, actually given a crap about what anyone else thought, let alone an almost stranger?

She nodded. "Very much so." Her eyes wandered around, settling on a much larger instrument sitting in the corner. "What's that?"

"It's a drum kit."

"Does it make... music, too?"

"It, uhm..." I chuckled a bit, drawing her attention back to me. "It does... Well, sort of, depending on whose standards you go by. On its own, it doesn't create all that much music, but it's an instrument with which you can administer rhythm. It's pretty essential to the kind of music I like."

"Can you show me?"

"You mean, can I play it?"

"If that's what you call it." She nodded, chewing on her bottom lip. Note to self: She definitely was more adorable than frustrating.

"I, uh, can make it make as much sound as anyone..." I smiled. "But we're not here to torture your ears. I promised it wouldn't hurt, didn't I? How about I just have Chuck show you once he gets here?"

Everything had always been wondrous to her, new and exciting, as if it hadn't been from this planet.

Or... like she had been a stranger to this world.

It was a thought that had occurred to me a little too late, but which now kept recurring, especially when my brain was taken over by alcohol, high percentages not referring to my brain activity, but the alcoholic strength of my poison of choice and, ultimately, my blood. Drunk me unquestionably had a tendency to let melancholy wash over him.

I wasn't sure how long I'd been sitting there, reminiscing, staring at the wall and drifting further away from reality sip by sip, but Jimmy's face appearing in front of mine made me jump. Literally.

"Oy, you shmexy beast. Let's find you a harrrrrlot," he smirked, enthusiastic and full of life. If someone filtered his blood for endorphins, adrenaline, or whatever controlled his moods, the result surely could have made for one potent energy drink or anti-psychotic. I should have probably tapped into his bloodstream myself.

"I'm not in the mood," I mumbled, tipping my bottle back again, trying to wave him away like he was a fly circling a pile of shit – the latter being yours truly.

"Then you obviously haven't had enough to drink. Let's find you some more of my favorite namesake, shall we?" He giggled like a little schoolgirl as his eyes drifted around the room.

"Have a seat, Jimmy." My voice was so serious compared to his, it made me sound like the priest to his Catholic schoolgirl. Pictures flashing through my mind of Jimmy in a schoolgirl's uniform *so* wasn't anything I wanted to ever have a repeat experience of.

"Uh-oh... Am I in trouble?" he asked, still chuckling a bit as he slumped down on the floor beside me.

"Why doesn't the Earth just fall down, Jimmy? I mean, I know *we* don't just fall down because of the Earth's gravitational pull. That's what keeps *us* in place. But what actually keeps the *Earth* in place?"

"Dude... Fuck. Shit. Maybe you *have* had enough – or even more than enough?" he mused, the chuckle still evident in his voice.

"Seriously, Jimmy. What if we're just part of one big crazy scheme? Like... maybe we're just part of a giant snow globe or some shit? And the only reason we move is 'cause someone keeps shaking it, repeatedly winding up what we're so damn accustomed to calling the universe—"

"Fuck my fucking mind... What the hell?!" Grabbing the bottle out of my hand, he took a big sip, shaking his head.

"That's why there's so much conformity, too, because we're alllll just part of a preprogrammed mechanism, and the ones among us who dare to be unique... They're considered errors." I looked at him with a grin. "You, my friend, are one big fuckin' error."

His mouth dropped open. "Gee... Thanks, dude," Jimmy mumbled, rolling his eyes. "Never thought anyone but my parents, or ex-girlfriends, would ever have the chance to call me a mistake. Not that anyone ever has. No one but you, 'my friend'."

"No, no, no, Jimmy. It's a *good* thing. Seriously. I *love* errors. I'm one of them. A big... fat... fucking... error. Part of a virus that seems to be eating its way through the whole fuckin' snow globe system. Part of what's blamed for making the whole thing pretty damn dysfunctional.

A hack gone wrong."

"What are you on, Owen? Do I need to call the nice men in white to bring you one of those 'love me, hug me' jackets?" He laughed, handing me back the bottle.

Great. I was trying to make sense of the mess in my head, and he thought I was drunk. Okay, maybe I was, but I hadn't bid all rational thought goodbye just yet.

Who.

The fuck.

Was.

I.

Kidding.

Snow globes.

Errors.

Ha. As if...

But I guess hanging by a thread did that to people. It made them imaginative, gave them reason to escape into their own little bubble for a while. To numb their feelings. To ignore the existence of the real world.

Chapter 3

"**F**ucking hell... I can't believe her!"

Mumbling, I stomped out of the garage. My little sister had some nerve. On more than one occasion, I had told her not to leave her stuff all over the garage – my garage. Now she could bid one of her most prized possessions goodbye. Knowing full well that she'd throw a fit upon her return, and hate me for it later, I smashed the piece of kitsch into the dumpster behind our parents' house, probably using more force than necessary, causing little shards of glass to shoot in different directions. The sound was absolute music to my ears and might have made me smile more than just a little bit. With that piece of shit gone, there would be no more unexpected hazards during band practice, for the time being anyway. The garage was my turf, and when my friends and I played, any and all objects on the floor posed a threat, increasing the chances of one of us getting injured. Broken ankles, cut feet, sprained wrists, and bloody noses weren't going to do us any good. Now that we were finally landing more and more local gigs and starting to make a name for ourselves, broken bones were the last thing we needed – unless, of course, we wanted to call ourselves "The Invalids". To be fair, worse names had been up for discussion, but that one would have just called for a career as a nursing home entertainment group, and that certainly wasn't for us. Granny panties on the mic stand and walkers in the pit... Nope, not what we envisioned.

However, my celebratory expression vanished just as soon as it had appeared, being replaced by a frown. Making my way back toward the garage door, I had heard a pained groan, prompting me to stop dead in my tracks.

Where had it come from, though?

I looked around, narrowing my eyes a bit to see farther – Seriously, why did we do that? I highly doubted it gave us 20/20 vision. It just made us look odd – but no matter what direction I turned, I couldn't see anything that would indicate somebody was hurt.

Mrs. Carter from across the street was out watering the lawn, seemingly fine, her movements as swift as ever. A guy a few houses down was getting into his car, but unless he was constipated or had to pass gas really badly, it wouldn't have made sense for him to be the source of the sound, either. It appeared to be just another regular day in the neighborhood. The sun was shining, the birds were chirping, the *sounds of a playground were fading into a distant background noise...*

And there it was again. A groan, followed by incoherent mumbling.

Following it took me back over to the dumpster – the scene of the crime,

if you will – and that was when I first spotted her... and the greenest eyes

I had ever seen.

"Hey... Good morning."

Her voice was soft and quiet, her words mere whispers against my ear. I felt her breath tickling the small hair on my neck, her fingers lazily trailing up and down my biceps, her leg moving in between mine, making my body stir.

"Mmm... Morning," I mumbled through a small smile, my voice husky, my mind still in that sweet state of oblivion you could only find yourself in right in between a dream too good to be true and reality setting in. With a content sigh, I pulled her body a little closer to mine, but her giggle soon dragged me out of my reverie.

Sure enough, the eyes staring back at me when I opened mine weren't the vibrant green ones I expected. They were a muddy brown, surrounded by freckles and curly red hair, rather than porcelain skin and a pitch-black, sleek curtain.

"You're not her," I stated absentmindedly as I sat up, disappointment evident in the tone of my voice.

Taking a deep breath and running both hands through my hair, I threw back the covers, picking up my clothes from the ones strewn around the room, carelessly tossing the rest onto the bed. She wasn't her. It hadn't been her. It had just been a dream. It fucking always was.

"What the hell's wrong with you?" the girl asked, eyes wide, almost sounding a little freaked out as she slipped on her shirt. "I'm not who?"

"I'm not *whom*," I corrected with a slight sigh as I got dressed, glancing at her over my shoulder. It looked like my words made her scoff in what I thought to be disbelief. I couldn't blame her. I wasn't even a hundred percent certain my version was the grammatically correct one. Truth be told, I was just incredibly annoyed she was who she was... or, rather, who she wasn't.

To be fair, my nameless conquest was adorable, especially with that confused, doe-like look on her face. Any other guy would have probably loved staying under the duvet with her for just a little longer, but I wasn't any other guy... and she wasn't *her*.

"I never would've pegged you as some kind of psycho," she mumbled under her breath, hastily putting on the rest of her clothes.

Some kind of psycho. Maybe that was what I was, or what I was turning into.

"That's because you don't know me, doll." I smirked, leaning onto the bed and bringing myself so close to her, our noses almost touched. "You accompanied a random stranger to his hotel room for some fun between the sheets. Let's analyze which one of us is the one with issues, shall we?"

"Of course I know you," she retorted, having the nerve to sound offended. "You're Owen Connors, singer, and sometimes guitarist, of The Cunt-Nuggets."

"You know the *image* of me – my name, my looks, how I sound. What I feel like inside of you, even. But you don't fucking know me. You see what you wanna see. An empty shell. An illusion."

The humorless laugh echoing through my words seemed to unnerve her even more. Hugging her jacket to her body, she warily climbed out of bed, careful to avoid any physical contact with me. Ironic, seeing as she'd just spent the night with me, wearing nothing but her birthday suit, and tried to come on to me again first thing in the morning.

"That's right, honey. Run as fast and as far as those heels will carry you," I said jokingly, shaking my head and grabbing a bottle, which had been knocked over, from the desk, taking the last sip. I could already see the hotel billing me for the most useless piece of furniture in the room.

Or maybe it was useful last night. That bottle sure didn't knock itself over...

"You're an asshole. And crazy."

She sounded as if she was close to tears, and for a short moment, I almost found myself feeling bad for her. Emphasis on *almost*. After all, she had undeniably made the mistake of falling for the mask, of willingly surrendering herself to me for what she must have been all too aware would only be a single night, not a lifetime of hot and steamy on the road romance.

"I'm well aware, thank you very much," I responded sarcastically, trying to figure out where I had tossed my pack of cigarettes the night before. "The beauty of it is that's what's expected of a rock star, though. The best of us either die young or go mental."

The sound of the door bouncing off the wall could be heard right after the word "die" had rolled off my tongue. *Rude.* She hadn't even given me enough time to finish my sentence before storming out. Not that I could blame her. I would have probably freaked out even the most diehard groupie with my half-sober antics.

Letting out a relieved sigh when I found my smokes, I lit my first of the day, ignoring the No Smoking signs the walls must have surely been subtly plastered with. Closing my eyes, I inhaled what would eventually turn my lungs into roads of tar, something that might end up being handy to ants once I was dead.

"'I'm tired of moving on...,' I sighed, trying to ignore everyone passing me by. The dry soil crunching underneath their feet caused me to shiver involuntarily, making it harder to keep my composure. I didn't know what it would feel like to be at war, but I was sure my emotional state must have come pretty close to that of a tired soldier fighting an epic battle against unknown enemies.

"Aiden, you know it's what's necessary if we want to at least try to ensure the ability of this planet to ever host life again...'

"'Stupid humans. It was all their fault. Sure, their ideas had seemed to work in the beginning. They had been able to find cures and vaccines, to breed new sorts of plants and animals. Then it had started to become too much, too much for them to handle, and some became greedy. It clouded

their better judgment... turning an initially good idea into something that went horribly wrong. For humans, it had always been more, more, more... until nature exhausted itself, until there was no more to take. Once that point had been reached, there was no turning back. It was too late. Natural resources became less efficient, supplies started to shrink. Our food was getting more rare, too, but what was nutrition compared to a human's most crucial need – oxygen, air to breathe?!'

"Owen! Are you even listening?" She chuckled, tossing a pillow at me, hitting me in the head. *I was perched on the floor, watching her, listening to her voice, taking in every feature – the way her lips moved with every word, how her chest heaved with every breath, the way her body vibrated when her words were accompanied by soft chuckles, the way her eyebrows moved when she put extra emphasis on a syllable.*

"Of course I am," *I smiled, grabbing the pillow and getting comfortable on it.* "You're talking about... natural selection or some other smart shit."

"Smart shit? That sounds like quite the paradoxical statement," *she laughed, shaking her head. Damn, she was beautiful.*

"Carry on, Ray. I'm all ears." *And even more eyes.*

Running a hand through her hair, she playfully rolled her eyes, but her blush betrayed her. She wasn't as immune to my charms as she liked to pretend.

"Let me know if I'm losing you though, 'kay?"

I nodded, making her smile. "Never." *And I meant it. I had no intention of ever letting her lose me, or of me losing her. Ever.*

She continued. "'Sure, yes, there had certainly been ways for humans to sort of manufacture oxygen – filter the air, do some chemical stuff, store the air to breathe in tanks... like at hospitals, or for people with severe respiratory issues. But nothing in life comes free. For most people, maintaining a living on artificiality had just become too expensive. Barely anybody could afford it anymore. As a result, we had to watch the human race start to cease to exist. They became one of those "endangered species" so often referred to in the animal kingdom. Let me tell you, it wasn't a pretty sight, even if we could do well enough without them, emphasis on if.

"'But it wasn't just humans, people like you, who had started to disappear. No. We all needed oxygen, so no matter how big or small an organism, you could see its numbers decrease day by day – some more rapidly than others, depending on their need for oxygen and other natural resources.

"'Those humans should've stopped while they still had the chance, before it all got out of control. Everyone was fine with their research and experiments, but taking it one step further and messing with the DNA of all things living? Not so much. They were supposed to impact things in positive ways only – to give life, to improve it, but not to take it. Their random words of comfort so often overheard meant nothing now, now that the world had been colored in fog-like shades of gray, green no longer the color of the majority of plants. Their changes called forth mutations, freeing plants of their chlorophyll, stealing their ability of photosynthesis, no longer enabling them to take care of the world's need

for oxygen. It was a risk no one considered until the storm hit.

"'The remaining scientists started trying their best to bring back trees as they had once been known to mankind, and the vast majority of the leftover population started to protect the environment to the best of their abilities in order to not make it worse.*

"We, too, did what we could, trying to spread as much of what was left of the "real deal" oxygen producers, not those aluminum foil-like gray poltergeists, to someday enable this planet, or at least this part of it, to be the host of life again. We could have, but probably wouldn't have cared less if we hadn't been so dependent on nature ourselves. As it was, we needed to save the planet – one ant at a time.

"'C'mon, Aiden. Stop daydreaming and help us spread and bury these seeds! Work ain't gonna get itself done, son!'

"'I could hear my father's voice calling from afar, but that didn't change the fact I wasn't exactly feeling like doing as I had been told.

"'I'm coming, Salvatore! I'm coming!' I replied rather dryly, rolling my muddy brown eyes.

"'Emotionally drained, but barely feeling any physical fatigue, I set one foot in front of the other, doing what we did best – working our little ant butts off. For the time being, we were left with a beautiful, once colorful world turned gray, with us – generations of us – left to pick up the pieces until we, too, might eventually cease to exist. We had to hope some human somewhere in this world might have a spark of intelligence left that would be enough to bring forth Generation Change, a generation that would bring things back to blooming in all ways possible.

"'I was well aware of the fact that saving the world was no longer a task for Clark Kent, Bruce Wayne, or Peter Parker. If we wanted to keep on living, we all needed to be a part of Generation Change. Saving, no... Rebuilding the world needed to be the mutual effort of all survivors, hoping for a better tomorrow. A tomorrow in which the planet could once again bloom with life – the most precious gift in the universe that would, hopefully, not be carelessly traded for greed this time because someday, there might be no one left to turn things around...'

"So... What do you think?" Rayven asked with a big smile.

"Did you honestly just say ant butts?" I chuckled, running a hand through my hair.

"Seriously? I read my whole essay to you and all you hear is the word 'butt'?!"

"What can I say? I'm a guy with this really beautiful individual sitting in front of him..."

"Owennnn..." With something in between a smile and a pout, she let her hair fall forward, all but hiding behind it. I could still see the color creeping into her cheeks, though. It was adorable.

"Rayyyyyyven..."

"Stop being mean. Please?"

"Oh, I don't think I'm being mean at all. You know, if you want me to shut up, you may just have to make me."

"Make you? You mean... with tape?"

Laughing, I rubbed my neck a bit, hoping she wasn't thinking I was laughing at her. In some ways, I may have been while trying to *figure out if she was being a smartass, or if she genuinely had no idea how much I wanted her to kiss me. Mostly, I was laughing at myself, though – at my once again failed attempt at moving our flirting to the next level.*

"No... No tape. Not yet," I finally answered, raising an eyebrow in anticipation of her response. There were so many remarks I could have made based on the mention of tape.

"I, uhm...," Rayven started, the pink hue of her skin deepening. Either realization had hit her, or not understanding me was making her feel uncomfortable.

"Never mind. What was your question?" Making her uncomfortable was the last thing I wanted.

"I... I think it was what do you think," she repeated, looking at me curiously.

When I didn't immediately reply, the memory replaying in my head, as if I were watching a recording, the question got repeated. To my dismay, the words didn't sound anything like the sweet voice I had let myself drift toward in my reverie.

"Earth to Owen... What do you think?" the disappointingly masculine voice asked again.

"About what?" I mumbled quietly, slowly opening my eyes to see Jimmy spread out on my bed.

"Oh, please. Don't be so overjoyed to see me," he chuckled. "I just bumped into your night's company stomping down the hall. Nice catch!"

"Not that I remember much of it." I shrugged, taking the last drag of my almost burnt-down cigarette.

"Figured. You were pretty far gone. You'd already started talking nonsense while we were still at the venue. Guess the drinks at the club afterward didn't really help."

"Humph... What did you want my thoughts on?"

"Are there any in your head?" he asked. While his voice dripped with amusement, his expression was concerned, maybe even a bit pitiful. Having friends who knew you well could be a blessing, but having best friends who knew you *too* well could also be a curse.

"You have no idea." I smirked, stretching and making my back pop. "I'm just not sure any of them would be on-topic."

"I don't even wanna know." He wrinkled his nose, letting me know his mind was way too deep in the gutter, something I definitely didn't want any elaboration on. So I didn't even dare asking what he'd read into my words.

"Well... Are you going to tell me what you came barging in here for or are you just going to take a nap? Or do you maybe want to cuddle?" I asked with the most charming smile I could muster. Like so many other times, my mind still being with her made it impossible to fully live in the moment.

"I'd love to take you up on that another time, sugar bear, but we were actually just wondering if you wanted to come to town with us. Trent wanted to explore the vicinity," Jimmy started, suddenly cracking up in the middle of his response. I suppose I looked just as confused as I felt. Shaking his head, he got up and opened the curtains that had eliminated close to all light. "Still daytime, lover boy. No worries."

I scowled at him. He was one to talk. It wasn't like he was trying to figure out the mystery that was the love of his life's disappearance.

Chapter 4

Exploring civilization with the boys was always interesting, to say the least. It didn't matter where we were – a small town in the Midwest, a world metropolis, or even our hometown – we always stuck out like a sore thumb. Piercings, tattoos, occasional funky haircuts, loud mouths, bad habits, partially strange clothing. We were every potential mother-in-law's worst nightmare. However, if you were one of the few fortunate ones in the inner circle and got to know us, we really weren't half bad.

"Hey, Chuck, how about some new heels?" Trent asked with a wicked expression, picking up a sparkly purple heel from an outside rack, bringing it so close to his face, one would think he wanted to take it to bed.

"You know, if they weren't sure to break within one night behind the drums, I'd totally go for them. I'm sure they'll have them in your size, though. You know what they say..." Chuck smirked.

"That a guitarist's fingers work it faster?" Trent chuckled, putting the shoe back.

"Thanks, man." Jimmy, our lead guitarist, grinned, slapping Trent's back in passing.

"And drummers hit it harder." Chuck nodded slowly. "Not sure what they say about keyboarders who occasionally pick up an acoustic guitar, though."

"I think they're said to have long fingers, an artist's hands," Jake chimed in. Trent frowned, which of course just cracked the rest of us up. We weren't just bandmates. We were best friends, brothers, family.

"You guys suck. Really. Turning my own joke against me." He pouted, throwing me a hopeful look. "What about vocalists?"

"I don't know, Trenton. We're good with our mouths?" I offered, giving him a crooked smile.

We hadn't been roaming the streets for long, but people who caught snippets of our banter were already staring us down. If I wasn't mistaken, one lady even crossed the road so she wouldn't have to get too close.

That's right, friends of the night. Go and lock up your daughters. You have another band of badmouthed rock stars stopping in.

Slowly losing track of the conversation, I scanned the windows of shops we passed. I wasn't looking for anything in particular, but my sister, Lyric, who ironically didn't have a musical bone in her body, loved it when I brought back little knick-knacks from each of the places the band visited.

Kitsch hoarder.

"My friend, the internet, says there's a place about three blocks down that's supposed to have bourbon burgers," I heard Jake say, the other guys not hesitating before agreeing to check the place out. Burgers and booze never sounded bad to any of us, so my mind naturally picked that exact moment to tune back into the conversation.

"Get me something that sounds good. I'll catch up in a few," I threw in, falling out of step with the others to go back to one of the little shops we had just passed.

"Want us to just wait?" Jimmy asked, eying me as if he were afraid I was about to run off. I hadn't become that distant and seemingly insane, had I?

"Nah. Go ahead. I just wanted to get Lyric a little something. I'll be right there."

Turning on my heels, I walked back to a shop that had a lot of really touristy things on display. *Dust catchers.* Things I'd never get for myself, but knew Lyric would love.

"Hey," I greeted the young woman behind the counter as I stepped in, letting my eyes wander around a bit. Nearly everything screamed for me to get out of there, but I was on a mission. I wouldn't fail my sister's need for memorabilia from places she had never visited.

"Welcome to Eastend's. Is there anything in particular you're looking for today?" she asked, sounding way too chipper for someone who worked in a place where unicorns probably went to take a shit.

What is it with people's need to add glitter to everything?

"Just lookin'." I shrugged casually, my gaze catching on the display covering most of the far wall.

"Are you a collector?"

I could feel her eyes on me as I approached the shelves, my hands in my pockets. I knew she probably thought I was an elephant in a china shop and was about to wreck the place, but the scenes playing out in my head as I eyed the incredibly huge selection of snow globes would take place in a more secluded spot... and not before I had paid for what I would destroy later on.

"I wouldn't say so," I murmured, unhurriedly running my finger along the edge of the shelf as I looked at the items in front of me. I couldn't possibly purchase everything they had in stock, so I had to select carefully.

My heart beating in a funny rhythm, I turned around slowly to look at the woman. "Do you deliver?"

"I... How much are you looking to buy?" she asked, clearly taken aback by my question. I supposed most people who walked into the shop left with only a bag or two.

"More than I can carry," I offered, my eyes dropping to her chest so I could get the name neatly written onto the little tag attached to her blouse. "Would that make the answer to my question a 'yes', Katelyn?"

"I'm sure something could be arranged." She didn't sound as sure as her words indicated, but I really didn't care, as long as I got what I wanted. What would have to happen behind the scenes to make that possible wasn't any of my business.

"Perfect." Nodding, I gave her my most charming smile before turning back toward the shelf. Chewing on my bottom lip in contemplation, I started picking out those worlds surrounded by glass, which had something familiar about them, placing them on the counter, one by one.

"These are beautiful choices." Katelyn smiled enthusiastically. I was certain she was already calculating the amount of money that would soon be charged to my card, debating if she could close early.

Transaction of the decade.

Had she known my plans for her precious decorations, she would have probably told me to take my business elsewhere.

"Look who finally made it!" Chuck cheered, motioning for the waitress, who immediately made her way over to the table and placed a beer in front of me.

"They've already ordered your food for you. Is that all right?" she asked with a smile she must have been getting paid to wear, even though her breasts were much more prominent than her face.

"Yeah, whatever. Thanks." I shrugged, taking a swig of the brew she had brought me as I watched her all but dance back toward the bar.

"So, what's for dinner?" I asked the guys. For some reason, Jake, the one who had suggested the place, looked almost sheepish, while amusement was written all over the other guys' faces. "Uh-oh... *Please* tell me this ain't one of those hipster places where all you can get with your organic beer is beetroot chips and peppercress."

"No." Jimmy shook his head, laughing. "But it turns out there's no such thing as bourbon burgers. Our friend here just missed the comma. They have bourbon *and* burgers, but unless we want a burger that had a bourbon bath, there's no such thing on the menu."

"Shut up," Jake pouted, throwing a crumpled napkin at Jimmy.

"Did you find anything for Owen female?" Trent asked with way too much interest, surely not just to do Jake a favor by changing topics.

I always suspected Trenton and Lyric were more than just friends, but I had yet to catch them doing more than exchanging hungry glances. Not that I wanted to catch them doing anything, but I couldn't even bust them texting each other.

I shrugged, pulling a small snow globe dangling from a keychain out of my pocket, holding it up.

"What's that? A glitter ball?" he asked, chuckling. "Let's tell Lyric you got her vampire testicles."

"Fuck. You." I shook my head with a roll of my eyes, bringing the bottle back to my lips and taking another big sip. "Maybe we should deliver *yours* on a hook."

"Not like she doesn't already have a grip on those," Jimmy laughed, earning death glares from both Trent and me. Maybe I wasn't the only one on to them...

"Took you quite a while to get that little thing," Trent mentioned, probably just trying to steer the conversation away from Lyric and him. Something for which I was exceptionally grateful. On one hand, I wanted to know what was going on, but on the other, she was my little sister... even if just by seven minutes and twenty-five seconds. Her sex life wasn't anything I wanted to hear about, unless I had some ass to kick – and then it better not be the ass of one of my best friends.

"Nah. I actually almost melted my credit card. The rest is gonna be delivered to the hotel." I shrugged, emptying my bottle just in time for the waitress to grab it as she brought the food to our table. "Didn't wanna cause any premature breakage."

"Premature breakage?" Jimmy laughed, my wording apparently enough to bring tears to his eyes. "What did you get? A deluxe blow-up doll with a 'gina to satisfy your every lonely night's dream?"

"Well, aren't you ever the poet?" I asked dryly, rolling my eyes.

"Guess that's a no to the plastic hoe?"

He almost sounded disappointed. I really wondered about him sometimes.

"Dude, that's nothing I would have shared with you anyway, so maybe that was a good bubble to burst." I chuckled, thanking our waitress as she placed another beer in front of me.

The way she made sure to lean over the table just a tad more than necessary made it more than obvious she was trying to assure we were aware of what she had to offer. However, it also made us, or at least me, painfully aware of the fact that she was desperate, and desperate chicks never floated my floatation device. They might seem to be all for a quick fun fuck at first, but once you buttered their buns, desperate dolls were the most likely to get clingy, needy, and whiny.

She seemed to have caught the attention of at least one of us, though. Chuck's eyes disappeared into her cleavage, but I wasn't looking for anything that couldn't be thrown out and sent on its way first thing in the morning. My objectification of women might seem crude to some, but I was always honest with every one of them, never promising more than a one-nighter. Honestly, more often than not, I hoped to be turned down. Should I ever have a daughter, I'd sure hope she wasn't that cheap and knew how to keep her legs closed.

"Guess we know what to get you for your next birthday," Jake chuckled, throwing one of his curly fries at Jimmy.

"I like 'em wet and warm, though." Jimmy smirked, popping the fry into his mouth.

"Guys..." Trent frowned, sounding utterly disgusted. "Please. We're trying to eat here."

"Not sure eating a doll is all too much fun. Is it, Owen?"

"How the fuck should I know, Jimmy? Do I look like I enjoy licking plastic?"

I glanced around, hoping no one was listening to the fucked-up conversation we were having. More specifically, I hoped no children were present. I was sure eating dolls had a different meaning to them, but I had a feeling it still would scar them for life.

"Aren't you the one who said vocalists were better with their mouths?"

Chapter 5

"**G**odfuckingdammit! *Fuck a fuckin' duck* three ways into the middle of next week! This can't be fucking happening!" I growled, shattering yet another one of my earlier purchases, forcefully smashing it in the hotel's back parking lot.

When it didn't have the sought-after result, I picked up my bottle of Jack, taking a few big gulps. The warm, fuzzy sensation the whiskey caused in the back of my throat was a heavenly relief. For a few short moments, it made me forget all about the puzzle I was so desperately trying to solve. It proved I was alive and conscious, that I wasn't just dreaming or imagining things. Maybe it wasn't exactly proof of the latter, but I sure as hell liked telling myself that.

After taking another few sips, I smashed the bottle, too, watching it explode as it hit the pavement, little shards of glass flying in every direction. If you were drunk enough, a breaking bottle looked like fireworks going off.

Maybe I should try flinging it at a streetlight or a neon sign next time.

"Excuse me, sir."

Turning to the gruff male voice, I realized the security guard's flashlight had probably contributed to the special effects of the flying fragments.

Neon sign it is then.

"What?" I asked, my tone indicating how little motivation I had to partake in a conversation.

"Hotel security." He raised the flashlight, shining it right in my eyes.

Dick, I thought, shielding my eyes with my arm.

"No shit, Sherlock. It's written across your left moob, and I'm sure you ain't wearing that fake police hat just for the fun of it."

I was used to being blinded on stage, but it was a whole different story when you were in a parking lot with a no-fun mall cop approaching you.

"Sir, some of the guests have been complai-"

"I *am* a guest."

"I understand, sir, but *other* guests aren't happy with the volume of your little... escapade."

"What the fuck were you expecting when you let rock stars lodge in your hotel?!" I asked a little too loudly, immediately regretting my words, despite my blood alcohol level. Our occupation's reputation preceded us, with trashed hotel rooms being the fear of every hotelier checking us in.

Way to be cliché, Connors.

"If you don't respect the other guests, I'm afraid I will have to ask you to leave – after you've cleaned up, of course."

"What if I don't?"

"Then I'll have to call the police. I am sure they'll be happy to provide you with a place to spend the night – courtesy of tax payers."

Oh, he had the nerve to get smart with me? I was sure my abs would have won against his moobs any time of the day. Maybe it was time to try a different tactic, though.

"But I'm not done with... this," I responded with a small pout, motioning toward the mess I had already made. He said I'd have to clean up anyway, so what would some more chaos matter?

"And what exactly is this?"

"I'm... It's... I am trying to find my muse? It's a very... essential creative process," I offered, nervousness and the lack of a cigarette causing me to bite my lip a bit. How did you explain the impossible to someone when your biggest mistake in life had been never believing in it yourself?

"In the middle of the night... by breaking things..." He raised his eyebrows, not even bothering to make his assumptions sound like a question.

Righteous bastard.

"If that's how you want to put it."

"Well, then, enlighten me. What would be your wording?"

"Finding a... creative outlet?"

"The only creative things I can find right here are your excuses. You have ten minutes," he mumbled, turning to leave.

"So I can keep going?" I really wished I didn't sound like a little boy on Christmas morning, but him not actually busting my ass gave me a new sense of hope. Not for understanding, or humanity, or any of that crap, but for finding *her*.

"Ten minutes and not a minute longer. Don't make me come back out here." What was probably supposed to sound like a threat sounded like promise to me – a promise of having about ten more chances of finding what I was looking for.

Smiling triumphantly, I turned back to the stack of boxes containing my purchases, picking up yet another one. Fiddling a little with the tape, then opening the packaging and removing the fitted Styrofoam shells, I soon held up the snow globe, letting the hotel's colorful outside lights reflect off it, making its insides glow and sparkle. They could be quite beautiful. I had to give addicts of kitsch, like my sister, that much.

Mere seconds later, though, the glass hit the ground, its shiny pieces flying about, its sparkly liquid slowly oozing across the pavement.

Ready for yet another beautiful disaster to unfold in front of me, I grabbed another one of the cardboard boxes, opening it. The treasure it held wasn't as intricate, but the world created within seemed somewhat familiar to me, so I hadn't hesitated to add it to my purchases.

Reaching my arm back as far as I could, I was just about to let it snap forward in order to hurl the snow globe when someone grabbed my arm, keeping me from flinging it toward the ground.

"Dude, what the fuck's going on with you?" Jimmy asked, carefully taking the ball-to-be-wrecked from me and setting it down with the other ones that hadn't been damaged. Yet.

"Nothing," I mumbled, my eyes fixed on my purchases, as if I had to guard them against any and all evil.

"This ain't fucking nothing, bro. You're a damn mess and you know it."

"I just... I..." Taking a deep breath, I ran both my hands through my hair, desperation getting the best of me. "I miss her so damn fucking much, Jimmy, it's driving me nuts."

"No shit," he scoffed, watching me intently. I was certain he was just waiting for me to lose it, to completely break down.

"You don't understand... It's like the Earth just swallowed her, like she disappeared into thin air."

"You've been telling her off for long enough."

He shook his head, actually sounding like it was my fault she was gone, missing. My fault. Mine. But I had never really told her off. I never would have.

Picking the snow globe he had taken from me back up, I didn't hesitate long enough for him to grab it again, smashing it to the ground. Nothing. Nothing but broken fragments... just like my soul.

"What the hell's this supposed to fix, Owen?"

"I'm trying to bring her the fuck back!" I replied, exasperated, feeling more lost than ever.

"Who?"

"Who do you think?!"

"Well, I thought you were talking about Destiny. But, clearly, you could just give her a call. Is this about...?" I heard realization dawning to him, wondering why he couldn't just say her name.

"She has a fuckin' nose, douche. She ain't the one 'whose name shall not be mentioned'."

Closing my eyes, I leaned against our bus, slowly sliding down until I hit the ground. I was mentally tired, like the ant she had once written about. I wanted answers, but how was I ever going to get them if no one dared to talk about her?

"She never called after she left, huh?" he asked, his voice dripping with pity and sympathy. I wanted neither one.

"She didn't just leave, Jimmy. She... She took her."

"Who?"

God, I loved him to death, but he sometimes sounded like a broken record.

"That lady. She said she was her mom, but..."

"You knew it was bound to happen, man."

Letting out a humorless laugh, I looked up at him. "Really? Enlighten me."

I wasn't pissed at him. I was pissed at the world, but mostly at myself because I seemed to be the only fucking one on the planet who didn't fucking understand.

"That's what exchange students do. Once their time is up, they leave. She always had that return ticket home," he explained calmly, his words accompanied by a small shrug

"Fucking damn it," I mumbled, rubbing my face. If only we'd told everyone the truth...

"Can we keep her?" I asked my mother as we waited for the doctor to be done tending to her wounds. Cuts that I had most likely caused when I'd thrown out my sister's piece of trash.

"She's not a stray cat, Owen. Finders keepers doesn't apply to people," Mom replied, her voice soft, concerned, rather than appalled.

"But she doesn't even remember where she came from." I frowned. "What if she has nowhere to go?"

"I'm sure her parents will be looking for her, if they aren't already."

"What if they aren't? Won't? What then? What if no one can find out who she is, where she's from, where she belongs? What if the records on her are as much a dead end as her memory?"

"I guess she'll go into the system then," my mother replied, shrugging a little, clearly not fond of the thought.

"Would you want that for Lyric or me? To end up in shitty foster care? Or a homeless shelter?" I asked, sounding like she had just made the most insane suggestion. And she kind of had.

"Why do you care so much?" she simply asked, her eyes searching mine.

"I... I don't know," I replied reluctantly, biting my lip a bit before quickly adding, "I don't care."

Truth be told, I had cared way too much – even then, when I had just found her, just met her. Something about her had always been different, intriguing, mesmerizing.

"What if people ask questions?" She sounded nervous as she paced the length of the living room, not able to stand or sit still for even five minutes.

"Well, you remember your name, right?" I asked, trying not to sound too amused by her discomfort, watching her every move.

"I told you already," she replied, stopping, looking at me like I was the one with amnesia. *"It's Rayven. Like the bird, but with a 'y'."*

"All right, Rayven with a 'y'. That answers the most obvious question." I smirked, my eyes never leaving her as she started pacing again.

"What's the second most obvious one?" She frowned, fidgeting with her fingers. I was amazed she wasn't stumbling over her own feet.

"How old are you?"

"Seventeen... I think. But I asked you a question."

"Which I answered," I chuckled, *"and so did you."*

"I... I suppose I did." She shrugged and nodded, swallowing. *"What else would they want to know?"*

"Where are you from?" I hoped asking her random questions was a way into the depths of her brain, maybe jarring some memory.

"I was made in China."

I frowned, tilting my head to the side a bit, slowly letting my gaze wander up and down her body as I let her words sink in. *"You don't* look Chinese."

She furrowed her brows. "I didn't say I was Chinese, just that I was made in China."

"What does that even mean?"

"I don't know... It says so on my foot. I saw it when I showered earlier. Why? Is that... strange?"

"What do you mean it says so on your foot? Take off your socks," I prompted, sitting up a bit straighter.

After we had gotten back from the hospital, we let her take a shower so she could get rid of that horrible smell from the dumpster, giving her some of my sister's clothes to wear. She hadn't mentioned having any tattoos, though. If you didn't have any memory, wouldn't a fucking tattoo stick out like a sore thumb?

"What? No!" she protested, acting as if I'd asked her to show me her boobs – which, for the record, I would have much rather taken a look at than her tools for walking.

"Oh, come on, Rayven. I've seen feet before. Sit and take off your socks. Simple as that."

"Please."

I blinked. "Please what?"

"You didn't say please," she said with a pout so small, it would have been easy to miss if I hadn't been paying such close attention to her every feature, her every move.

"Dearest Rayven, would you pleeeeeeease be so kind as to sit your ass down on the sofa and take off those socks?" I offered, giving her the most charming smile I could muster. I let out a relieved breath when she eventually did as she'd been asked.

Gently grasping her ankle, I lifted her foot to take a look. I shit you not, she actually had the words Made in China tattooed on the bottom of her foot, the ink a faded grey-black.

"Huh... I guess you could tell people you are from China, but you might want to twist the truth a little and not tell anyone about that... mark."

"Why?" Irritation plastered on her face, she pulled her foot away, carefully putting her socks back on.

"Because no one tells people where they were conceived... and no parent writes it all across their kids. Just... Tell them you're an exchange student or something. My sister's doing that exchange thing over in Germany right now. You could be her... exchangee, I guess. Seems to be a good story to sell."

"So... I'm Rayven, I'm seventeen, and until I remember, I am an exchange student from China, the counterpart to your sister?"

"Yup. Sending a kid away, taking a kid in. As soon as Mom gets the paperwork done, that's what we'll tell people. But not just until you randomly remember. You can't just change a story like that and slap people in the face with the truth. We'd have to come up with a different story then to, you know, wrap up nicely that we lied."

I gave her a small smile, happy I'd been able to, more or less, talk both of them into the arrangement, as well as a somewhat believable cover story.

"She never was an exchange student, James," I mumbled, wishing I hadn't destroyed my bottle of whiskey along with the snow globes.

Such a waste of Jack.

"What do you mean? Didn't she live with your family while Lyric was abroad?"

"Yeah, but... We didn't pick her up from no airport. I found her in the dumpster behind my parents' place." I looked up at him slowly, seeing his lips twitching.

Suddenly, he doubled over laughing, holding his stomach with one hand as he wiped his eyes with the other. It probably was the reaction that had to be expected. Truthfully, though, I had hoped he would end up asking a question or two, helping me make sense of it all, instead of cracking up.

"C'mon, Owen. I'll take you to bed. You're so shitfaced, it's not even funny."

"For not being funny, you sure laughed hard enough," I mumbled, glaring at him. If looks could kill, he would have had to have more lives than a cat to still be standing there.

"You just never struck me as a funny drunk before."

"Oh?" I rolled my eyes a bit as I grabbed his offered hand, clumsily pulling myself up. "What kinda drunk have I struck you as then?"

"Well... The horny kind?" Clearly trying to hold back his laughter, Jimmy looked as if he were about to explode.

"The lettin' go-go kind?" A sad little smile tugged at my lips, never reaching my eyes. The alcohol usually helped me remember a little less, numbing the pain.

"Don't start singing now, but yes, I suppose that'd be one way to put it."

"Not in the mood to sing anyway." I shrugged, almost stumbling as I stopped on the stairs leading up to the hotel's back door.

"What now?" Jimmy asked with an overly dramatic sigh, making me want to slap him senseless. He wasn't allowed to be dramatic when I was the one whose last hour had involved too much drama for a Spanish telenovela.

"What 'bout my balls?" I pouted, attempting to take a few steps backward, glad he was holding me so I didn't face-plant into the pavement.

"I keep wondering the same thing, man. Guess you lost them on our last stop."

"Fuck you!"

"Right here, right now?"

"You're dumb."

"And you're drunk. You know you love me," he chuckled, slowly guiding me into the hotel and toward the elevators.

"Don't let anyone touch my balls!" I called out to the security guard as we passed him. I still had plans for those. They'd be joining the others in snow globe heaven in the morning. I was on a mission, drunk or not.

Once Jimmy had maneuvered me into my room, he gave me just enough of a push to make me fall face-first into my pillow.

"Hmm, stay," I mumbled, cuddling into the fluffiness as Jimmy worked on getting me out of my boots.

"Didn't know your flags flew that way now."

I heard my shoes hit the floor, or maybe the wall, before the bed dipped next to me, the impact of his weight making the mattress curve down. Jimmy wasn't fat, he was somewhat lanky, but he was one tall motherfucker. I couldn't help wondering if his feet dangled off the end of the bed. However, now that my body had touched the warm, comfortable softness, I was way too lazy to move.

"Dick," I mumbled into the pillow, my lips tugging up as I shot the insult at him.

"I got one. Wanna see?"

"Ewwww, gross. No. I got my own. Thanks, though." I chuckled.

Before I knew it, my hoarse laughter turned into broken breaths, then silent sobs.

"Shit. Fuck. Are you *crying?*" Jimmy asked, appalled, sounding as if it were the most impossible and inappropriate thing he had ever witnessed.

"No." I sniffed.

"Stop lying, shithead."

"It's not lying when the answer to your question's fucking obvious," I said, a little too loudly for my own ears. I pressed my face into the pillow in an attempt to stop the tears before they could escape my eyes.

"All right, all right. C'mon," he mumbled, pulling me against his chest only moments after having made a dumb joke about being gay, yet I couldn't bring myself to push him away. Maybe I needed to get it all out once and for all, although I highly doubted it would help any.

"The snow globes... They...," I started to explain, failing to find words that would sound reasonable to anyone but myself.

"Don't start with the whole puppet master theory again, Owen. You know that's absolute bullshit."

"No, you don't understand...," I mumbled against his chest, pulling away and putting my head back onto the pillow to keep things from getting too weird.

"Break it down for me then?"

"Rayven... She..." Taking a deep, faltering breath, I trailed off as my thoughts drifted back to the first time I had talked about said theory... and that time, I had been dead sober.

"Are you all right?" Rayven asked quietly as I lay in the grass in the front yard, her almost silent footsteps coming closer. If she hadn't spoken up, I probably wouldn't even have noticed her approaching.

"No," I mumbled, my voice barely above a whisper. How could I be?

"I'm sorry. I feel like this is all my fault," she whispered as she joined me, laying her head next to mine, her legs stretching out in the opposite direction.

"It's not, not really. This has been coming for a long time." I sighed, staring up at the stars. "We're just too different, and Destiny doesn't like

different. She never has. She's all about conformity and being cool... whatever that means."

"Then why were you with her in the first place?" Her voice was soft as she turned her head just enough to look at me.

I gave a slight, barely noticeable shrug. Damn, I would have loved to kiss her right then and there, but I didn't want her to feel like she was a rebound.

"It just kinda happened. I've realized that Destiny might be Destiny, but she sure as hell ain't my destiny."

Acknowledging my words with a nod, she faced the beautiful night sky again. Wishing the atmosphere weren't so melancholic, I got really close to begging her to turn her gorgeous face my way again.

I sighed. "You know... Moments like this make me think about choices, failures, disappointments, why we do what we do the way we do it."

When I heard a chuckle, I shot her a look, shaking my head. I was trying to be serious for once, but she seemed to think I was joking.

"I'm sorry. It's just... That almost sounded like you were about to start rapping." She apologized, trying to suppress her amusement, which made a hint of a smile flicker across my face, despite everything.

"Gee, thanks, Ray. Glad you remember what rap is, but I was being serious." I took a deep breath. "Like... why doesn't the Earth just fall down? I mean, I know we don't just fall down because of the Earth's gravitational pull. That's what keeps us in place, attached like a magnet. But what is it that actually keeps the Earth itself in place? I'm sure *there is some scientific explanation that I was taught at one time or another when I wasn't paying attention, but... What if, maybe, we're just part of a giant snow globe? What if the only reason we move at all is because someone keeps shaking up what we're so used to calling the universe, pulling the strings? And that's why there's so much damn conformity, too, because our choices aren't really ours and we're all just part of a mechanism, a scheme. And the ones amongst us who dare to be different, who make mistakes and step out of line, who can't be assed to give enough fucks to pretend being someone they're not, someone they don't wanna be? They're errors. Unwanted mistakes, messing things up."*

"Owen... Where's all of this coming from? Are you drunk?" she asked, concern straining her voice. I could feel her eyes searching my face.

"Oh, come on. I'm obviously one of them," I answered with a humorless laugh. "A big... fat... error. Part of a virus that seems to be eating its way through the whole snow globe system. Part of what's blamed for making the whole thing so damn dysfunctional."

"Owen..."

"I know. I know. Who the fuck am I kidding? Snow globes. Errors. Ha. But you know what? I guess hanging by a thread will do that to people. It makes them imaginative. Gives them reason to escape into their own little bubble for a while, to numb their feelings and ignore the existence of the real world."

"Is that why you came out here? To... ignore the real world for a while?" she asked softly, sounding as if she were afraid to ask the wrong questions. Did I really seem that vulnerable and breakable? Guess

Destiny had really done my head in.

"Yes."

"Do you want me to go? Leave?"

"No."

She sighed. "Ladies and gentlemen, may I introduce the King of Monosyllabism."

"Hey, watch it, Queen of Linguistics. I just gave you a pretty big speech," I replied, unable to hold back a smirk.

"More like a rant, you mean."

"Whatever, smart ass," I mumbled, reaching back and wrapping my fingers around her hand in a moment of courage, squeezing softly. "Thank you."

I was instantly distracted by the electric surge her touch seemed to send through my body as she turned her hand so our palms were touching.

"What for?" she asked reluctantly.

"Being there... here. Making everything better by just giving a shit."

I ran my hand down my face, taking a deep breath, trying to collect my thoughts. "Rayven and I... We've had that same conversation before."

"Did she tell you off like I did?"

Judging by his smug expression, he wouldn't have expected anything else from her. She had always been somewhat fierce, speaking her mind, barely ever seeming to possess a working brain-to-mouth filter... which was just one of the many things I had loved about her.

"Not really, no," I mumbled. "She actually believed in my words even more than I did." I smirked as I remembered.

"Rayven... I didn't mean all that snow globe shit the other day. It was just a crazy rant, nothing more. You can't seriously think that's where you came from. A fuckin' glitter ball? Next thing you'll try telling me is that you don't have a belly button..." I was infuriated. How the hell could she even come remotely close to reckoning that any of my stupid ramblings were true?

"Don't ridicule me. Of course I have a belly button," she said defensively, looking at her feet for a moment – to gather what was left of her courage, I guessed. *"The other day, when you were talking about all that snow globe stuff, I... I had this weird sense of déjà-vu. I shrugged it off because, honestly, realistically speaking, it made absolutely no sense."*

"You're right. It doesn't."

"But I kept having these dreams afterward. There was... I remembered feeling some sort of earthquake. The next thing I knew, I was in that dumpster behind your house – waking up right after you'd smashed your sister's snow globe. Wouldn't it make sense for me to have ended up there because–"

"Stop talking, Rayven. Just stop. Why are you trying to make up such a ridiculous story about your... origin? By now, I understand you wouldn't want to tell me where you're from – even if you remembered. I get it. I've stopped asking. What else do you want? Who the fuck cares?"

"I care, Owen. I do. I thought you did, too... well, about me anyway."

"I do, Rayven, a whole fuckin' lot. It's just... How could you possibly believe a stinking snow globe brought you here?"

"That's exactly it, Owen. Believe. Why is it so hard for you to just believe?" she asked, close to tears, her voice shaking. It shattered my heart to see her like that.

"Because this ain't no fuckin' fairy tale, Rayven... if that's even your name. This is real life with all its fucked-up moments. It doesn't give you a break just because you 'believe'!" I roared, almost spitting the words at her.

"I'd be your break if you'd just–" she started, but I interrupted her before she could get too far.

"If I just what? If I just 'believed'?" I threw in, all but sneering the last word.

"No, Owen. I... I was going to say if you'd just let me," she responded quietly, seeming more lost than the day I had found her in the dumpster.

"What?!" he asked, obviously labeling her more crazy than he thought I was.

"She... Rayven... She believed me." I looked at Jimmy in silence for a moment to gauge his reaction. He was either a good actor or couldn't quite wrap his mind around my words because his expression was as blank as an empty canvas.

"She... believed you," he slowly repeated. "As in being convinced there's little people living in balls made of glass and filled with liquid and glitter?"

"Yeah... and she thought she was one of them," I mumbled, the thoughts of her more sobering than any cold shower or hot cup of coffee.

"Rayven thought she was a little person from a snow globe world?" he repeated dryly, earning another stare of daggers from my side of the bed.

"Yes. That kind of believed. She even gave me a name. A name she believed her little town had been called."

"Which was... What? Snowmania? St. Balls?" He chuckled, having way too much fun with it all. "Seriously. What did she say the name was? I'm curious."

"Snowden."

"So now she's a spy? Guess that makes sense, considering the whole walls made of glass kinda thing."

"That was post-Rayven and you know it," I sighed, turning onto my back, the ceiling suddenly becoming more and more interesting to look at than my friend. I knew he was trying to be there for me, but was somewhat failing because he found humor in my every word, making me feel as if the drunk/sober roles had been reversed.

Chapter 6

The following few days crept by slowly, yet seemed to be passing in a blur at the same time. After having destroyed nearly $1,850 - $1,847.83 to be exact, minus whatever Lyric's little gimmick had been – worth of collectibles behind the hotel that night, *and* having to pay for clean-up, I had come to the realization that my hopes of finding and freeing someone caught in a snow globe had been a ridiculous idea. Almost like cutting open your dad's tennis balls hoping to find a Pokémon inside one of them. Not that I'd ever done that.

"Earth to Owen. You listening, man?" Chuck asked, throwing his napkin my way. It barely missed my plate as it went tumbling to the floor. Gross. Knowing him, he had probably used it to wipe away chunks of buggers right before deciding it was time to send it flying like a paper plane.

"Depends. What am I supposed to be listening to?" I asked, shoving my loaded chopsticks into my mouth. Chinese food hadn't been the same since she'd left. It seemed to always come with a side of bitterness, but a couple of the guys loved it. Even though I wanted to, I couldn't always take a rain check when one of them suggested going for some Cheng Du Chicken, Chow Mein, or Mu Shu Pork.

Not like any of that can be found at the next best burger joint.

"Lyrics," Jimmy smirked, although I could see the concern in his eyes. The breakdown he'd witnessed probably made him think he had to monitor me somehow.

"Lyric's what?" I asked, frowning a bit before looking at Trent, pointing my chopsticks at him. "If this is about any of Lyric's body parts, used for procreation or not, I don't even wanna hear a word."

"God, Owen, get your head back in the game." Jake chuckled. "Lyrics as in a song text. 'Cause you know we're a band, right? Making money by making music? We were pitching some ideas for the next album. What planet has your mind run off to?"

"You don't wanna know," Jimmy threw in, shaking his head. Yup, he was definitely trying to make my mother proud by monitoring me.

"Maybe we should call the next album *Rayvenous*," Trent mumbled before taking a sip of his drink, glancing at me out of the corner of his eye. "Give him an outlet and coping mechanism once and for all."

Swallowing hard, I looked at him, feeling like someone had sucked all the oxygen out of the room. Either the guys had all gone quiet, or my mind successfully shut out every single sound in the room.

Rayvenous... How ironic. Ravenous for Rayven. Her name kept delivering more and more puns for wordplay, yet none of them hinted at where I could find her. Maybe Trent was right and I needed to find a way to let go. Music had always been my outlet. Just like Rayven had once said, it was what feelings sounded like. So why the hell not.

"Dude, don't hit him," Jimmy ground out, obviously misinterpreting the look on my face and the silence it had been accompanied by. Judging by the other guys' expressions, he wasn't the only one thinking I was ready to unleash my inner fury.

"Hit him?" I chuckled, shaking my head, running a hand through my hair. "I was actually gonna say I like the idea. Whether it'll be released or not, maybe it's exactly what I need."

"For real?" Trent asked, slowly eying me, apparently still fearing I might lose it.

"Yeah... As much as I don't want to let go, it's been years. Maybe it's time." I shrugged, feeling a melancholy wash over me. Letting go meant admitting it was over... and over was the last thing I wanted it to be.

"Guess it'll be an album for the lovesick and the broken-hearted then. Or for the obsessed." Trent smirked, still looking sympathetic.

I'd always known her disappearance hadn't just had an impact on me. It had ripped apart my heart, taken away a piece of me, which consequently was something my friends and family had to deal with.

They'd lost her, too, but loss was a douche that made you feel self-centered, easily convincing you others couldn't possibly miss someone as much as you did... especially when that person was the center of your universe.

"We'll see."

I shrugged again, grabbing a fortune cookie, my mood and expression darkening infinitely after I cracked it open. They should have called those things misfortune cookies or bullshit biscuits instead.

"Which of you fucking horsecocksuckers thought this would be a fun prank? Huh?!" I roared, crunching the two halves of the cookie in my fist. "Which one of you wants to get his ass kicked so hard, you won't be able to sit for a year?"

My friends looked at me as if they thought I was on the verge of needing to be admitted to an asylum. To be fair, I was pretty much ready to tar and feather the next person who made the wrong kind of remark, so maybe a padded cell wouldn't have been the worst place to spend a couple nights.

"Dude, the waitress brought those over with our meals. I swear to God, none of us had anything to do with whatever your little note says," Jimmy said, using his calming, "think about it" voice as he reached for my fortune, which I quickly snatched out of his reach.

Fuck no.

Like a generic little saying could coincidentally hit the bullseye like that.

"You don't even believe in any kind of god," I mumbled, my eyes searching their faces. One of them had to have done it, and whoever had must be the devil incarnate.

"Whatever. Okay then. I swear to all the grain farmers in the world... because I *do* believe in whiskey. A whole fuckin' lot. Always been the answer to all my prayers."

"Shut the fuck up, Jimmy. Trent, is that why you started that *Rayvenous* bullshit? To get me going?"

"What? No," Trent replied, shaking his head. "I was sincerely serious about that. *Sinceriously.* How about telling us what that note says?"

"*Maybe it is time to stop looking and let go. Lucky numbers: 8, 27, 11, 13,*" I read, glaring at each one of them. I ran a hand through my hair in a way that made me feel like I was pulling half of it out in the process. *Guess I really am starting to lose hair over her.*

"Wow...," Chuck mumbled, his eyes on the table. Was he feeling guilty and needed to avert his gaze? "That's crazy."

"I'm serious, guys. This shit ain't funny," I said desperately, plopping back down into my chair. *When did I stand up? Way to draw every single person's eyes to you, Owen.*

Jimmy frowned. "None of us are laughing, Owen. I don't think any of us would be cruel enough to play that kinda prank." He pulled the little piece of paper out of my grasp. "Do the numbers mean anything to you?"

"I... Today's November 13th. August 27th was her birthday... Well, the day of her arrival."

"Her birthday? Or the day you guys picked her up?" Chuck asked.

Apparently, he still had some catching up to do, even after all these years.

"*Happy birthday.*" *I smiled, handing her a mug cake, something my sister had taught me to make. It was easy enough for me not to mess up.*

"*Uh... What?*" *she asked, clearly confused, slowly bringing her nose close to the cup she now held. I had always told her I was no good in the kitchen, saying nothing I'd ever made was enjoyable – actually, I think my exact words were "not survivable". Thus, her reaction to the chocolatey goodness in her hands came as no surprise. It was as if she were trying to figure out if I was trying to kill her. Admittedly, it was a strange kind of adorable.*

"*Happy birthday? You know, the day you entered this world?*" *I eyed her as I tried to keep my amusement at bay. Despite how fucking perfect she was to me, she had a tendency to get somewhat self-conscious whenever she felt like someone was making fun of her. I wasn't, but I didn't want her to start feeling uncomfortable.*

"*You don't know when my birthday is.*" *Her frown and the way she furrowed her brows made my smirk widen, my dimples probably popping in their full glory... which I was only even aware of because she had once mentioned thinking they were cute.*

"*That's why I said 'the day you entered this world'. My world. That has to be worth celebrating.*"

My words made her nose wrinkle in the cutest way. She was probably trying to show disdain for the whole situation, but she couldn't manage to hide the twinkle in her eyes. She hated being the center of attention. Too bad for her, though, because she most definitely had been the center of mine since the first time I saw her. Whenever we were in the same room, nothing and no one else mattered. Even when we weren't in spatial proximity, though, she was the main occupant of my mind.

"*I, uh... Thank you?*" *She finally smiled hesitantly, sending unexpected butterflies throughout my whole body.*

"What's the damn difference?" I asked, closing my eyes and letting my head fall back. "This is a fucking joke."

"Now I'm curious, though," Jimmy mumbled. I could hear the plastic wrapped around his cookie rustle. Seconds later, he started cracking up. "*Soberness welcomes you. It will become you.* I don't get *that* drunk *that* often... although I guess I did just call whiskey my religion. Go ahead, Trent. Your turn."

"Knowing my luck, it probably says something that'll make Owen want to kill me." He sighed as he reached for one. Despite everything, it made the corners of my lips tug up. Reading the slip of paper he had retrieved from his cookie, he shook his head. "Yeah, fuck that. I ain't telling. This shit's dumb. I'm not gonna dig my own grave here."

"If you aren't, I will." Jimmy chuckled, reaching for the paper. After a little fight, Trent gave it up, and Jimmy looked as if he'd just won the lottery before grimacing a little. "*Lyric is a beautiful thing.* Yeah, man. You're fucked."

"Dude, it does *not* say that!" I frowned deeply, extending my hand so Jimmy could hand me Trent's fortune. Upon reading it, I felt like my eyes were about to pop out of my head. "What the hell...? Okay, time to fess up, guys. My bet's on Jimmy. So far, his has been the least... personal."

"Hey, it pretty much called me an alcoholic," Jimmy countered defensively.

While his little line had been the least likely to make him feel like he was getting kicked in the face, I had to admit that he probably had the biggest heart of us all. Yes, he was a prankster, like all of us when we were together, but he wouldn't have played us with cruel intentions.

"This is creepy. I really wanna go," Jake mumbled. He glared at the fortune cookies, as if trying to will them to stay away from him. Unfortunately, none of us had ever received our letters to Hogwarts, so the art of magic wasn't something any of us were proficient at.

Chuckling, Chuck was the next one to open his. "*Next time, pick the chicken.* See, nothing out of the ordinary."

"Yeah, boring. Unless it's trying to tell you that you could use some protein," Jimmy suggested cheekily. "You know, it's supposed to be healthier for you?"

"Are you calling me fat?" Chuck smirked back, cocking an eyebrow.

"Never, darlin'... although Chunky Chuck would be a fun stage name." Jimmy shook his head, his eyes wandering back to Jake. "Come on, dude. Your turn. Saving the best for last, as always."

"No." He shook his head. "I'm not touching that thing. It'll probably tell me I'll get run over by the bus at the next stop, or that one of you has used my toothbrush to clean the toilet. Yours have all been too close to the truth for me not to get paranoid over *whatever* it will say."

"Your turn," Jimmy repeated in a sing-song voice. "Don't be such a puss. Bet it predicts you'll get royally fucked by a unicorn."

"Great. Bet that wouldn't hurt at all."

Grumbling, Jake reached for the cookie he had been glaring at, jumping, quickly pulling back his hand when Chuck made a barking sound.

"Fucktard," he mumbled, carefully opening the wrapper. Cracking the cookie, he popped one half into his mouth before reading the words, almost choking on it.

"That bad?" Jimmy frowned, but only got a mix of a shrug and a nod in response as Jake took a sip of water. "Hurry up, man. What does it say?"

Jake cleared his throat. *"Eloping is fun. Maybe you should consider a renewal for your friends and family, though."*

"Your fortune's full of crap," Jimmy pouted, his eyes widening when Jake bit his lip and looked away.

"You did not," I uttered, surprise in my voice. "You and Katie? When?"

"On the tour last year. You know, when we were in Vegas."

"Shut the ever-loving fuck up!" Jimmy laughed. "You got married in Vegas, while we were all there, and you didn't say a fucking word?! Not even afterward?"

"We agreed." Jake shrugged. "I don't even think she's told her parents."

"But we're not your parents," Jimmy replied, the pout back on his face. "You didn't have an option with them, but you handpicked us motherfuckers. *Bros before hoes*, they say, and you didn't even do *hoes with bros*." Frowning, Jimmy must have realized how that sounded. "Scratch that. You know what I mean. We should have been there. Holding your hand while you peed, showering you with strippers the night before."

"Fuck. I hate Chinese. We really should agree to never have dinner here ever again," I mumbled, our waitress stopping by to see if we needed anything else at that exact moment.

"The food not good?" she asked in broken English, frowning. By the look of it, she was debating whether she should be offended or indifferent.

"The food was great, but... Who makes these cookies?" I asked, holding up the wrapper of my fortune cookie to make sure she knew what I was referring to.

"Oh, fortune cookie? Comes from big factory in big box. Generic. Make many a day." She shrugged. "They cheap. You want more?"

"No!" we all said pretty much in unison, causing the waitress to flinch. She must have thought we were either crazy or shitfaced to the max.

"Sorry I ask. I bring check," she said quickly, walking off before we could have forced her to engage in any more conversation.

Once back on the bus, I taped my fortune onto the wall next to my pillow. While Trent and the cookie might have been right, that it was time to let go, I couldn't move past the fact that all our fortunes had been so... accurate. A fact that, of course, made me want to do the opposite of what it had suggested. Despite the musings of the past few days, having more or less successfully tried to make myself believe that snow globe land had been nothing but a myth, a product of my imagination and a whiff of insanity, those cookies threw me right back into believing that maybe, just maybe, the impossible was possible after all. I mean, what were the chances of five guys getting pretty accurate fortunes? Whether Chuck's had been fitting or he'd been the one to mess with the messages, the cookie wasn't the first to mention he should pursue a healthier lifestyle – something he most definitely would not have told himself, not even for the sake of an alibi.

And just like that, with one tiny piece of paper telling me to move on, letting go had once again become that much harder.

Chapter 7

Officially, there were approximately 7.5 billion people in the world, although I was sure that was inaccurate even just ten seconds after that accumulated number had been announced... except for maybe in some extremely coincidental moments when the numbers of those coming and going were exactly the same. Other than that, though? How could it be? People were born, people died, and people disappeared all the time. Nobody cared.

Unless, of course, it affected them. Directly. Indirectly. At all. When it did, their world came crashing down, and not even a fraction of those 7.5 billion people mattered to them anymore. All that did was the one person gained... or lost.

At that very moment, nothing rang more true than the saying, "To the world you may just be one person, but to one person, you may be the world."

———•◆•———

"'Sup, shithead?" Serena smirked as she let herself fall onto the sofa next to me, the cushions puffing out air as if unhappy with being squished.

"Go away," I mumbled, glancing at her out of the corner of my eye, hoping I didn't look quite as pouty as I felt.

"You forget this is *my* shop, Mr. Doom-and-Gloom. To what do I owe the pleasure? Anything in there catch your eye?" She nodded at the sketchbook in my hands.

Going from giving me shit to talking business in less than a beat... Only Serena.

"Been thinking 'bout adding a dermal to the raven's eye. Maybe some green sparkle to give it some life." I shrugged, flipping through the sketchbook I had started looking at while she was with a customer. Having some time off before our next shows, the guys and I all went back home for a few days. Naturally, my first stop was Serena's.

"Ever gonna tell me the story behind that one?" she smirked, starting to pull up my shirt to look at her latest mark on my skin.

"Nope," I simply said with the slightest shake of my head.

I usually didn't mind telling her why I had a certain image in mind. It helped her come up with the perfect design... or so I thought, not that my mind worked like that of someone who knew how to work a pencil, let alone a tattoo machine. Letting her inch up the fabric, I moved my arm a little so she could have a closer look. It wasn't like she was seeing any of it for the first time. I was her canvas, and it didn't bother me any to be treated like it.

"Shit, I love it. It looks great, don't you think?" She smiled, leaning back a bit to admire her work. Some might have considered her self-praise to be inappropriate, but she was one hell of an artist. The best, if you asked for my two cents, so it was well-deserved.

"You know I do," I chuckled softly, turning just enough so I could look at her. "Unless you stop working your magic, I won't let anyone else color my skin ever again."

"N'awww, Owey, that's the cutest thing anyone has said to me all day. One could think you're hitting on me." She smirked, wiggling her eyebrows as she let go of my shirt again.

"Don't call me that," I groaned, almost sounding disgusted at her cutification of my name, "and you know I'm not."

"So... Why the dermal? Thought you didn't like anchors."

"I really don't, but I think it would add to it. Enhance it? Whatever you wanna call it. Didn't know I needed a reason."

"Mmm-hmm," she mused, pressing her lips together in a tight line before shrugging her tiny shoulders a little. "I don't know. If you don't like the bling and decide to remove it again, it'll probably scar the picture. I'd absolutely hate to ruin it."

"Hmm, yeah." I frowned. "Didn't consider that... but I don't care. I may not usually be into that kinda stuff, but I just want it to look even more full of life. Make it *beyond* perfect." I smirked, figuring the discussion would be over sooner rather than later if I buttered her up a little more.

"Well, if you're sure." She smirked, sounding almost a little too excited about getting to manipulate my skin further. "I *do* think it'd look great, but that's something you really gotta decide for yourself. I know the ink I've given you is forever, too, and a dermal *is* easier to remove. But it's your choice and your choice alone, rock star."

"Speaking of ink... I want more of that, too."

"Now?"

"Whenever you're free. We're here for a couple of weeks, then we're doing a few stops across the States before hopping up to Canada for a few days. After that, it's Europe for two months. I'd obviously like to get it done before we hit the road again, but if it doesn't work with your schedule, or you don't have the muse, we can do it once we're back again."

"What?! No! I always have the muse." She blew a strand of currently bubblegum-colored hair out of her face. "I wanna do you. Now." Her eyes widened a little as a wicked smile spread across her face. "But not in the way I just implied. I think."

"Right," I chuckled, pulling a crumpled piece of paper out of my pocket, handing it to her.

"Prepared as ever," she sighed dramatically. I knew she preferred to be told what somebody wanted, but if something wasn't easily explained, a picture said more than a thousand words. She looked at the paper, then at me. "Jeez, who got you whipped?"

"Wouldn't it be who *had* you whipped, if anything, considering its state?" I asked with a roll of my eyes, gently tapping my finger on the sheet.

"I s'ppose." She shrugged, biting her lip a bit. "Where do you want it? Your heart's pretty much already covered now."

"Close-ish. Not right underneath because I got plans for that. Kinda thinking under my left shoulder blade?"

"So... Somewhat close to the heart, but behind you, as if in the past?" She smirked. "I like it. But you don't want it in that purple-pink color, do you?"

"Color-wise, you can do whatever you want. You know I'm more into black-and-white or gray scales, but if you think something else would look good..."

"Rainbow!" she exclaimed, as if she'd been waiting for me to ask her opinion.

Great. No way.

"Fuck you, Serena. Shattered or not, I'm not having you tattoo a rainbow-colored heart on me."

"Party pooper. Spoilsport. Shithead."

"Love you, too, Serena, but no. Not in a thousand years."

Not even half an hour later, the familiar buzzing of the machine, which seemed massive in Serena's delicate hand, calmed my nerves. Spread out on a piece of furniture that could have promised a relaxing massage if in a different business, I couldn't wait for the scratchy feeling of the needles pushing ink into my system. I was more than ready to let Serena get under my skin... in the best way possible.

"Ready, fucktard?" she asked casually, as if calling me by my given name. Sure, that wasn't too far off some days, but I couldn't recall having pissed on her parade that day... yet.

"This better come with a happy ending," I replied with a smirk, giving her a quick glance over my shoulder before settling into a more comfortable position again.

"Doesn't using my hands always lead to one?" Serena chuckled, taking the bait. In another life, someone like her could have made an amazing girlfriend, but in this one, she just wasn't for me.

"Just don't end up sneezing or having a spontaneous seizure. Wouldn't want it to look like I got tattooed by a drunk trucker while he did the waitress on a bar's basement's pool table," I mumbled into the crook of my arm, which I had comfortably folded under my head.

"I'm sure that was supposed to sound like sarcasm, or maybe a joke, but shit, dude. You sound like a fuckin' kitten," she retorted with a chuckle.

"Laughing's also off the table, Ser. No wibbly-wobbly-humpty-dumpty lines."

"Wibbly-wobbly-humpty-dumpty?" Serena asked amusedly, thankfully putting some distance between the needle and my skin before cracking up. "You *did* just sign the waiver saying you weren't drunk or under any other influence but that of a broken heart, right?"

"Thanks for making me sound like such a wuss." I tried to sound sad, failing miserably when I couldn't hold back my own laughter.

"Well, I hate to break it to ya, no pun intended, but I *am* making sparkling shards of shattered glass magically, but permanently, appear on your skin right now."

Serena smirked as she lowered the machine's vibrating tip until it repeatedly penetrated my skin, and I was almost a hundred percent certain she was enjoying the process as much as I was. After all, her job was as driven by passion as mine.

"So what colors did you decide on back there?" I asked curiously after a few moments. After I had shot down her suggestion of adding vibrant rainbow colors to my back, we hadn't discussed the topic any further. I fully trusted her artistic instincts, but that didn't mean I wasn't impatient to know, and see, what she was adding to the canvas I called skin.

"You'll have to wait and see, but I know you'll love it."

I didn't even have to look at her to know what kind of expression she wore. I could hear the triumphant smile in her voice, and it didn't take a rocket scientist to figure out that Serena found joy in the smallest and strangest of things.

"It better not look like unicorn puke," I mumbled jokingly.

"Don't worry. No rainbows. We settled that issue," Serena

chuckled. "I'm female and an artist. I listen and get inspired by anything and everything."

"Wow... That sounds like I have the most boring, monotonous office job there is. No creativity needed," I smirked, gently shaking my head, cautious not to move too much so I wouldn't ruin her artwork.

"Nah, although I'm *pretty* sure you've found, and lost, your one and only muse, which you're wearing figuratively on your sleeve, literally on your skin."

"Lost, huh?" I asked, swallowing hard. I was aware of her inquisitive tone. She was prying, once again attempting to find out more about the girl who had not only inspired most of my lyrics ever since high school, but also the majority of my tattoos.

"Maybe I only misplaced her."

"I'm not saying she took all your muse and inspiration with her when she went... wherever she went, whenever and whyever, but I've known you long enough to know that it's all coming from one place, whether you want to openly admit it or not."

"That almost sounded like a rant. Anything else you wanna say?" I almost wished she'd stop her work for a moment so I could turn around and look at her.

"I'm not jealous, if that's what you're getting at." Serena sighed dramatically, but I could hear the smirk back in her voice. "I just wish you'd tell me more than 'There once was this girl who stole my heart.'"

I chuckled. "I've never said that."

"With every song you've sung and every stencil I've applied, you have."

"How poetic of you. Maybe you should write our next song. I'll make sure you get an extra-special mention on the album," I replied sarcastically. There was only so much questioning I could take in the day regarding Rayven. Serena had reached her limit. I was sure she felt just about as smart and knowledgeable about the topic as she had before, though.

"Am I not getting that anyway?" she asked, sounding pouty. "I mean, hell-ooo." She cleared her throat. "'The biggest thank you, however, does not go to any of our families. It goes out to Serena, whose buzzing needles have serenaded and sedated me long enough for my head to swim with lyrics, chords, and dance moves. She actually inspired the mic stand hump and that hip swing that always makes y'all's heads spin. She's the reason y'all are getting what you're getting, so all those flying panties and bras... Serena's the one who should take the credit.'"

"Oh god, move that fuckin' machine. I'm dying here," I said through clenched teeth before laughter erupted from my lungs. Luckily, she knew me well enough to have already stopped inking my skin as the last words left my lips.

"Is that a no?" she asked, sounding like my sister when I had told her she was no longer allowed to hang out with the guys and me because she had started growing boobs. Think what you want, but teenage boys and a starting-to-be boobie sister among them? Nope to the nopey-nope.

"Uh... yes. No. I mean... I don't know." I chuckled, turning onto my side so I could get a good look at her. "That little speech of yours right there actually deserves a mention. Maybe you should write it down. Not, you know, on my skin, but on paper. With a pen. So I can remember every word when it comes to composing the acknowledgments."

"Really?" She smiled sweetly, shoving my shoulder with her free hand. "So adorbs, Owen. Now, turn back around and lay down before I decide I have to sit on you to get my work done."

"Pretty sure I was as serious as you were." I complied, although I wouldn't exactly have complained about her sitting on me, either.

Where the fuck did that thought come from?!

"So... One hundred and one percent?"

"Minus the same amount," I chuckled, getting comfortable again.

"I might just turn this thing on your back into a pig's ass. A pig that forgot to wipe."

"You wouldn't do that. Ever. You love what you do too much. Plus, I'm pretty sure pigs *never* wipe."

"Shut up. I like you better when you're whiny, rather than smartassy."

I could tell she was trying to sound dry, although her attempts were a waste of energy. I was sure even a deaf person could have sensed her smirk.

⸻ ◆ ⸻

"All righty, matey. Ready to see yer new'st?"

"Hmm?" I asked, stifling a yawn. I had started to doze off and was surprised I didn't feel like there was drool on my chin. Then again, the bed might have simply absorbed it. Call me crazy, but to me, being tattooed was one of the most relaxing feelings there was.

"Seriously, Ow? You missed my wannabe Scottish pirate accent?"

"I'll get you a parrot to make up for it." I smiled lazily, sitting up and stretching a little.

"You'd make a great tattoo model. Maybe I should take you to my next convention. Not only would I be bringing a star, it'd be a hot one at that... Ka-ching!"

"I feel so used. Like a piece of cheap meat." I sighed, trying to sound hurt. There generally wasn't any way you could be serious around her.

Tattoo Therapy 101 by Owen Connors: Enjoy it. Every moment of it. No matter if it's the before, the during, or the after.

"You're premium Angus, baby," she chuckled, her eyes roaming over my bare chest.

"That look ain't helpin'." I stood in order to get a look at her newest piece of art. "And you couldn't come up with anything better than 'premium Angus'?"

"Mirror, Mirror, on the wall. Who's the bestest of them all?" She smiled, ignoring my question, proudly passing me a hand-held mirror so I could check out my shoulder in the wall mirror without having to contort my body.

"You are, my queen," I joked, letting my eyes take in each and every freshly colored patch of my skin. Clean lines came together in an intricate design – a shattered heart, each of its dark pieces reflecting light, like shards of glass. She couldn't have translated my idea any better.

"No one more bestest?" She smiled as she grabbed everything she'd need to wrap up my ink for the next few hours.

"No one I know of. I'm like a loyal little puppy when it comes to my tattoos. Ever since your marker touched my skin for that first stencil, it's been all yours."

"Aww, that's probably the cheesiest thing anyone's ever said to me." It was obvious she was trying to keep from laughing as she batted her eyelashes at a hundred miles per hour.

"You might want to step up your love life then." I regretted my words as soon as her shoe hit the back of my knee. I winced. "Gee, thanks."

She started wrapping my tattoo. "You deserved it, cockhead. You don't get to pick on other people's love life when you don't even have one of your own."

My face fell. "Touché, Serena. Touché."

"I... I didn't mean it like that," she said quickly, sighing a little. "I mean... I did kinda, but–"

"It's fine."

"No, you're being monosyllabic, so it was obviously something someone with the emotional IQ of a potato would say."

"I'll just call you Curly Fry from now on," I offered with a lopsided, half-hearted smile, pulling my shirt back on.

"I actually like curly fries, though." She frowned, making my expression soften.

"Yeah, me, too."

Chapter 8

"**Well, well, well. Look who's** decided to join us!" Jimmy yelled through the bar as I entered, as if me joining the rest of the band was a rare occurrence.

Once I got close enough for his words not to raise the attention of every other person in the bar, Trent smirked. "And look at his face. Is that an afterglow I see? Did someone finally get some?"

It was Friday night, so the place was buzzing with mostly college kids, who just loved to share things that were none of their business all across every social media outlet out there.

"If you're referring to more ink, the answer is yes." I smiled proudly, standing tall, chest out, as if I had just told them I'd gotten laid by half a cheerleading squad.

"You... got another tattoo?" Trent asked, not doing a good job at hiding his disappointment, if he were even trying.

"We may just have to get a cheese grater to rub all yours off if you're suddenly going all anti-ink." I chuckled, my eyes dropping to the tattoos covering his arms.

"Nah, man. Just saying... I had hoped you'd gotten laid."

"Better."

"Better? Dude, I love getting tattooed as much as the next guy, but it doesn't beat hot and sweaty, lustful and passionate, loud, core-shaking, skin-smacking, wall-banging, bed-breaking sex."

"Core-shaking, skin-smacking, wall-banging, and bed-breaking?" Jimmy threw in, shaking with laughter. "Where'd you pick that one up? *50 Shades of Wordporn*? Fanfiction?"

"Never know. Serena might've given him a hand... or something." Wiggling his eyebrows, Trent pretended to be jerking off an imaginary dick.

Disturbing.

"A tattoo and a dermal. That's all I asked for, and it's all she gave me." I rolled my eyes, my tone dry, hoping it would intercept the direction in which his train of thought had been heading.

"A dermal?" Jimmy asked, leaping for that piece of information like a lion stalking his prey, waiting for the perfect moment to strike. "Snake eyes?"

"What the hell are snake eyes?" I frowned, his look making me feel as if I'd been living under a rock for the past decade or so.

"I don't think you can get dermals on your cock, man. He'd be better off with an apa or a prince or something. More useful, too." Chuck grinned.

When did my friends become experts on... sparkly decorations of the nether regions?

"Mmm-hmm. I'm sure Serena would be all over that. She's always had a thing for little Owen. I'm sure she'd love *big* Owen, too." Trent chuckled.

I wasn't sure where that analogy had come from. I was fairly certain I'd always been bigger than my dick. I wasn't now, nor had I ever been, a fucking tapir. Their dicks were long enough to scratch their own backs. About nineteen inches. Actual inches, too, not the homonymous measurement unit made up – and used – by males all around the globe.

"Wait for it..." Jimmy smirked, holding up his fingers as if getting ready to count to three.

"We're just friends."

I rolled my eyes when Jimmy pumped his fist in the air. Apparently, that was what he'd been waiting for. And just like that, Serena's words echoed through my mind.

I'm not jealous, if that's what you're getting at.

"I think..." I added, shrugging. I ordered a beer from the waitress, who I was sure was putting on an extra big smile for us.

"Whoa... Where'd that come from?" Jimmy chuckled, clearly not having expected that afterthought. "Something happen while she was getting under your skin?"

Literally.

"Nothing out of the ordinary. Where's Jake?"

"Probably doing what we thought you were doing," Trent smirked. "You know... catching up and catching crabs."

"Dude, you're gross. *You* are obviously the deprived one. Go and get some."

What I said didn't register with me before the guys were all but crying with laughter. Face paling, I shook my head slowly.

"Never mind. Don't. I'm not ordering you to get into my sister's pants. Ever. *Eww.* No. Stay deprived. Get nothing but blue balls. Hell, get black ones for all I care."

"Come on, man. You know Lyric and I are–"

"Uh-huh... Just friends...," I interrupted, using the same tone I always used when I referred to Serena and me. However, there was one big difference. I had never even seen Serena naked, whereas I was pretty certain Trent and Lyric had been trying to sneak around behind my back for a while now, unsuccessfully, knowing I would never approve of my twin sister dating a fellow musician.

Why? *Please.* Because I *was* one. I knew how crazy being on the road could get, and I wasn't sure Trent could keep it zipped for anyone but his hands for months at a time while Lyric waited for him at home.

"What if she says pleeeease?" Trent asked, frowning when I shot him a look.

Why did he have to go and dull my glow?

———— •◆• ————

A few too many drinks later, I fell into bed and lazily kicked off my shoes, not bothering with any other articles of clothing. I just couldn't care less.

Burying my face in the cloudy softness of the pillows in my childhood bedroom, I was sure I could still smell Rayven on them. She had loved all things pomegranate, and her hair always had a fruity, but not too sweet, scent to it.

Sighing deeply, I closed my eyes, wondering where she was, what she was doing, how she was doing... hoping there wasn't a *who* involved in all the things she was doing. I wanted her to be happy, wherever she was, but I also wanted her to be happy with me, not some Chinese guy who didn't even speak her language and served her cats and dogs for dinner. She had always loved little felines – but to cuddle them, not eat them.

Turning over, I rubbed my hands over my face. A sob story wasn't what I needed. I needed to find a permanent way out of my misery. It had been years since I last saw her, and there was no sign of her ever returning. I mean, surely they had paper and pens wherever she was, so she could have contacted me, even if she were somewhere she didn't have access to a computer. Shit, she could have sent me an owl or a message in a bottle for all I cared.

Hey, you up? I texted Serena, my mind making decisions my heart didn't agree with, my thumbs acting of their own accord as they punched in the words. Misery loved company, right? Wasn't that what they always said?

I don't offer my services to drunk people, the screen read a few minutes later.

You just made yourself sound like a hooker, Serena.

After that, there was nothing for what seemed like an eternity. God, I had grown to hate waiting for a reply when the ball was in the female's court. Maybe I suffered from a mental disorder... like PTRED, Post-Traumatic Rayven Experience Disorder. Yup. That must have been it.

Is that what you want me to be? she finally replied.

I read and reread her message several times, making sure I grasped her meaning. Had she just offered...?

Uh... What? I replied, dumbfounded. She couldn't have. We didn't like each other that way. Or was it why I had texted her? For a booty call? A way to forget, even if just for the night? Distraction was a remedy that never really did its job. A pill you regretted taking. A fix that never lasted.

Are you looking for someone to make you scream?

Okay, she was just messing with me now. She must have been. There was no other explanation for it, so why not go with it? Good-natured banter between two friends... After all, it was what we were used to.

In every language I speak, I replied after a moment, taking off my shirt and tossing it toward the corner of my room – just like I had when I was seventeen. Must be about being where making a mess could actually aggravate someone. Not that my mother particularly cared at my age.

And how many is that?

Shaking my head in amusement, I loosened my belt to get more comfortable, ready to pass out, despite the unusual topic of our virtual conversation.

One – but that's beside the point.

The longer it took for her to reply, the happier I was she hadn't. Yes, my original train of thought made me extremely horny. I could feel myself straining against the fabric of my shorts, held captive by the rough material of my jeans. But it wasn't her I longed for. It wasn't Serena who drove my lust. Just like the past few years, it was *her*. Rayven. As much as I liked to pretend I could forget about her for even just a little bit, it had never worked. Even when I was inside of someone else, she was all I could think about. Serena deserved better. They both did. Add in the fact I didn't want to ruin the last memory I had of her in that very bed with me, and even my drunken self was smart enough not to act on what Serena suggested.

"Owen, stop!"

The sound of her laughter was better than any music I ever had the pleasure of listening to – and that was saying a lot, considering how much I loved music.

"Or what?" I smirked, softly digging my fingers into her sides, tickling her as she tried scooting out from underneath me, but I had her perfectly pinned to the mattress of my bed.

"Or I'll... I'll kick you," she offered breathlessly, obviously fishing for the right thing to say, her words sounding like nothing but an empty threat.

"You wouldn't," I chuckled, acting on a moment of bravery and letting my hands slide underneath her shirt, my fingers sprawled across the soft skin of her stomach. I'd happily keep tormenting her if it meant I could indulge in her careless giggling just a little bit longer.

"You're right. I wouldn't," she agreed quietly, seeming even more out of breath than before, although I was no longer tickling her and she was no longer laughing wildly. In fact, the only wild thing was the beating of her heart, radiating from her chest to mine... and, admittedly, my thoughts.

In a matter of seconds, the atmosphere went from lighthearted to buzzing with energy, tiny currents shooting through every fiber of my body like little electric shocks. Judging by the way her breathing had changed, she felt it, too. The little flicker of her tongue moistening her lips was all it took for mine to be magnetically pulled to hers.

The instant our lips touched, it was like they were moving in sync. It didn't take long for feather-light kisses to turn frantic, pent-up need – and a whole fucking lot of want – pushing to the surface. Breaths turned into sighs, then moans. Clothing vanished and all inhibitions were lost, her hands, her lips, her whole body sending waves of–

"What the ever-lovin' fuck?" I groaned as I pulled my hand out of my pants, the waistband of my shorts snapping back to reconnect with my skin, sending a welcome sting through my body.

My phone, which wouldn't stop buzzing, had definitely ruined one perfectly set-up orgasm, courtesy of all things Rayven. As I reached for it on the nightstand, where I had tossed it when I had put my hand to a different use, I mentally cursed myself for not having turned it off altogether.

"What?!" I barked into the receiver, not at all happy with whomever had felt the need to interrupt. Of course, I could have checked the caller ID, but my blood supply wasn't exactly circulating in my brain at that moment.

"Hey, Owen," Serena purred, a breathy, almost nervous chuckle underlying her voice. "You stopped answering your texts and, well... I didn't want to ring the bell and wake up your whole family."

"What do you mean 'ring the bell'?"

"Oh, you know, this little round, white button next to the door that goes ding-dong when you push it?"

In any other situation, I would have laughed at her using the word "dong".

Some things just never get old.

"Serena, I... I didn't ask you to come over," I mumbled, squeezing my eyes shut and running a hand through my hair in an attempt to straighten out my thoughts. Yup, nope, my blood was still mainly occupied by a body part farther south than my head... at least the head most commonly used for thinking.

"But I'm here now, and it's raining, and–"

"What's your point?" I probably sounded a little harsher than intended because the other end of the line went silent for a moment.

"I'm wet."

"That's what rain does."

"Maybe I was referring to places not directly impacted by rain. There's only one way for you to find out."

"Serena..."

I probably sounded like a whiny puppy, but I didn't give a shit. Part of me just wanted her to go away, to leave me alone, but the other part urged me to go let her in, to make her finish what I had started right before she had so inconsiderately dialed my number.

"If you let me in, we could bet on how many different ways I can make you say my name in a set amount of time..."

"Let's see... There's annoyed, rejective..."

"Did you just say *erective*?" she asked, giggling as if she had actually really misunderstood me and thought it was the most disturbingly charming thing she had heard all day.

"Serena...," I sighed again. Against my better judgment, I got up.

"Can you at least not be a dick, although I am sure you have a magnificent one, and let me in? Pleeease?"

"Promise to keep your hands to yourself." Never would I have thought I'd ever say those words to a girl. Ever. Especially not one as attractive as Serena. She was every bit my kind of girl... and wasn't at the same time.

"I will not, under any circumstances, force myself on you."

While she sounded sincere, I didn't hear her make any promises. Still, I made my way down the stairs and to the front door, hanging up the phone as I opened it. I ran a hand through my hair again, wearing nothing but my shorts, not attempting to hide the tent I was sporting – and not even feeling remotely sorry about it. She had come over unannounced, and I wasn't exactly voluntarily inviting her in. The courtesy of looking presentable was reserved for visitors I actually wanted.

"I see I have some work to do," Serena smirked, letting her hands slide down my chest as she bit her bottom lip, her nails digging into my skin gently. She started pushing me back toward the stairway.

"Serena...," I warned, my voice strained, my mind confused, my body... Well, that was even more full of want now that it had physically connected with an actual soft, female, boobed human being, who I was sure had the matching, fitting parts in her supposedly wet pants.

To be fair, making out with her would have one big advantage over it being some dingy girl found at a random bar. She was the one who had recently marked me, so she would be well aware of the areas of my body that were off limits, of where to stop her nails from scraping along my skin before they'd catch on the shiny green ball screwed onto the anchor she had driven into my skin.

Shiny green... Shit, what am I even doing?!

"Ssssh," she smirked, getting onto her tiptoes in an attempt to get her lips closer to mine as my feet hit the bottom stair. "You'll wake everyone up."

"We can't. *I* can't."

"From what I can see, you most definitely can, and I'm pretty sure you haven't exactly been abstinent since high school."

She sighed, defeat audible in her every syllable. I was grateful she took a small step back, hoping it would give me a chance to get all my ducks in a row while I silently told my dick to lay low.

Duck, dick, dickady duck... duckady dick... dick, duck, duck, dick... fuck duck dick duck fuck...

While my mind decided it was time to have some immature fun with words, induced by whatever amount of alcohol was left in my bloodstream, I couldn't help but chuckle, rubbing a hand down my face. *Shit.* At least laughter usually was a good anti-bonerous medicine, though.

"What's so funny?" Serena asked, crossing her arms, eyeing me. She must have been convinced I was going absolutely nuts. Not only had I turned down her advances, but I was also starting to laugh maniacally.

"Nothing," I offered half-assedly, running a hand through my undoubtedly disheveled hair. "Wanna go somewhere?"

"Like where?"

"Meadow Heights? We can take one of our friends, Jack or Jim... or whatever else my Dad has around. Maybe even some Berry and Jen's?"

"You mean *Ben and Jerry's?*" she scoffed.

I was sure she thought she could hear the last of my marbles hitting the floor. Good thing the house had carpeting – and even better that I could feel my *ego* deflating... so to speak.

"Yeah, sure, that. Whatever."

"Just how drunk are you? You sure you haven't hit your head? Meadow Heights, booze stolen from your dad's stash, ice cream containers... Feels a hell of a lot like you're going *17 Again* on me."

Pouting a bit, I looked at her, crossing my arms. "Is that a no?"

"No, Owen, it's not." She sighed, biting the inside of her cheek in contemplation.

I knew hanging out, getting wasted, and devouring ice cream wasn't exactly what she'd come over for, but it was all I could offer. Even under the influence, I was nowhere near ready to let her step in to take care of... pressing issues.

Had she shown up right after her first text, before my mind had wandered off to blissfully reminisce about Rayven between my sheets, would I have shamelessly abused the moment?

Fuck yes.

But it was a fine line between those moments of *Fuck it, fuck me* and those of *If only she were here – and only her.* It was a line so fine, stepping from one side to the other took no time at all. Sometimes, I felt as if my balls were bipolar. To say it was a constant up and down would have been just a little too literal.

At the same time, though, that line oftentimes was fine enough to blur, and that was usually when I fucked up. I didn't want that to happen where Serena was concerned because I actually valued our friendship far too much to ruin it for a short-term pussy and a pair of by-the-hour boobs, which was all anyone after Rayven had been to me.

Just a quick fuck.

A short-term solution.

"Hell-oh? Earth to Owen. Are you listening?" Serena asked, snapping her fingers in front of my face, as if I were a Golden Retriever that hadn't been sitting still long enough to receive his treats.

That automatically had my eyes dropping to another, even greater and somewhat related t-word – her tits.

"Unless, of course, you want to take me up on the offer after all. We can still stay, go upstairs..." She smirked, her eyes sultry, apparently satisfied with where my gaze had landed. I swear she started squeezing her arms together just a little bit more to give her boobs a push-up effect no padded bra ever could.

"Uh... No. My train of thought just... derailed," I mumbled, popping my neck from side to side, forcing my eyes to lose focus on her cleavage and allowing them to settle on her face again. "Sorry. You were saying?"

"I was saying that you should probably go get dressed and grab whatever poison you want to indulge in. I'll drive. I don't want your sorry, half-drunken ass to pretzel us around a tree," she replied amusedly.

Despite my self-inflicted blue balls, I couldn't be happier she seemed to be taking rejection so good-naturedly, instead of throwing a fit over me not ravishing her on the spot when she'd all but thrown herself at me. At the same time, though, her behavior was a little confusing and rather unnerving. Did she act like she didn't care so as not to appear vulnerable? Or was making a pass at me a bet, perhaps even some twisted kind of test?

————◆————

After Serena pulled her beat up pick-up onto a dirt road and parked, we got out and got comfortable in the bed of the truck. While it was probably handy for camping trips and romantic stargazing adventures, which we were most certainly not on, I thought it was an old piece of junk... but Serena had always emphasized that it wasn't. According to her, it simply had "character" and "history".

Meadow Heights was a little hill overlooking the city. You could escape the noise without feeling so country you had to listen to girls in white lace dresses and cowboy boots singing about every boy they've never had. You could just sit, enjoy the view, and...

Realization hit me the moment I lifted the bottle to my lips to let another sip of the amber liquid slide down my throat. Meadow Heights... or *The Kissing Hill*, as it was most commonly referred to by tweens, teens, and everyone who wasn't quite at the peak-level of adulting just yet, which was one of the reasons I had never taken Rayven there. It would have simply seemed too much like a meaningless fling, which it had never been.

Almost panicking, I turned to look at my colorful friend, who had the grace to laugh at whatever my expression was conveying.

"You chokin' or something'?" she asked amusedly before frowning, all color draining from her face. "Oh God. Oh God, oh God, oh God... *Please* tell me you're not going to throw up, especially not in, or on, my truck. Just... Don't... At all. I can't stand the smell, sight, or sound of someone puking. Not even dry-heaving. Don't do it. I can't deal with it."

"Relax," I chuckled, tension leaving my body when I realized her thoughts weren't heading in the same direction as mine. "Just wanted to make sure you knew I hadn't suggested Meadows for the... sex of it."

"Sex of it?" she repeated with a giggle. I couldn't help wondering why I had even brought it up, considering I wasn't planning on getting into her pants, or letting her into mine. "They may say that the hills have eyes, but... I've never heard of them having sex before."

"Mmm-hmm." I took another swig from the bottle to keep myself from making an inappropriate comment that would have been sure to get her mind back into the gutter – probably to the point of no return.

"Don't worry. I got the message when you pushed me back, despite more than obviously being ready to be... taken care of in each and every way known to *man*kind," she said teasingly, softly nudging me.

I mentally willed my dick to stay put and not react to her words. It – figuratively – sucked, my body feeling so disconnected with my mind and, most importantly, my heart. Serena wasn't fooling anyone, either. She might have tried to act tough, as if none of it mattered, but I was certain I had seen disappointment and sadness flicker through her eyes. For a moment, I couldn't help but wonder just how long she had been... crushing on me, but I got sidetracked by a little creature crawling across the cool and smooth metal surface between us.

Wordlessly, I shoved the bottle at Serena, capturing the little bug. I held up my hand, twisting and turning it just enough to always keep the bug in sight, my other hand underneath it like a safety net to prevent it from vanishing into the night.

"What the fuck are you doing? It'll sting like hell when – and not just if, but when – that little shithead ends up taking a piss on you!" Serena shrieked.

I had to try my damnedest not to laugh at her. The knowledge that she was freaked out by an animal not even the size of her fingernail would surely come in handy at some point in the future.

"Haven't you ever wondered their purpose? As tiny as they are...," I mused, Rayven's short story from her creative writing class in high school echoing through my head, as if she were sitting right there with us, excited about the words she had brought to life.

"Uh... Other than annoying the living hell out of me during the summer? No. Ants are nasty little things," she scoffed, wrinkling her nose, taking a noticeably small sip from the bottle, looking at me and my little friend in disdain.

"Let me tell you a story then." I smiled proudly as I started to recite Rayven's story, trying to recall every word in order to stay as true to the original as I possibly could with the alcohol clouding my memory.

When I was done, Serena looked at me with wide eyes. "Dude, that's some poetic shit. Alcohol turns you into a weirdo." She laughed, using her index finger to flick the ant off my hand.

"Hey!" I pouted. "You're causing an antopocalypsos! The end of the world!"

"You sure that wasn't a syllable or two too many? I think you meant apocalypse."

"I dunno. I think I'm getting drunk." I shrugged with a cheesy smile, but I wasn't sure if it were because of the alcohol or because of the memories shooting through my mind like fireflies on crack, wrecking my synapses and messing with the sanity I had left.

I woke up in my bed, curled into a fetal position... naked?

Naked, but alone. In that instance, alone was good, even if it made me question the nudity, as well as the identity of the person who had been thoughtful enough to tightly close the curtains and place a bottle of water and some painkillers on my bedside table. I glanced over, seeing the trash can next to my bed.

I must've been really shitfaced.

Sitting up just enough to gulp down the bottle of water in an attempt to erase whatever taste had made itself at home inside my mouth, I tried to recall the events of the night before. I remembered Serena showing up at my door, ready to jump my bones, and asking her to take me to Meadow Heights... Everything that might or might not have happened after that, aside from telling her a story about hard-working ants, had been eliminated from my memory. Using the part of my brain that had already woken up and was, at least somewhat, ready to function, I tried piecing together bits and pieces of the night.

Had I lost my willpower and given in to Serena after all?

Had she dropped me off at a bar? Had I brought home someone else? Had I turned her down, only to give in to a stranger?

Had my mother heard me come in and taken mercy on me, making my room hangover friendly? It sure as hell hadn't been my sister, even if she was home from college. That little monster would have done the exact opposite, leaving me a note that would have said something along the lines of *I hope you suffer, sucker*.

Either way, though, none of the options ghosting through my head would have explained my lack of clothing, let alone none of it being strewn across my bedroom floor in the unorderly fashion of drunk stripping before diving into bed, be it by myself or with somebody else.

"Well, this'll be fun," I mumbled to no one but myself as I ran a hand through my hair, forcing my aching body out of bed. Not getting drunk to the point of no remembrance ever again would have been an amazingly awesome promise to make to myself, but I was aware that wouldn't ever happen, so I figured I should do myself a favor and save myself the disappointment. God knew I'd gotten my fair share of that without causing it myself.

After slowly pulling on a pair of shorts and a t-shirt, which had passed the sniff test, I stumbled down the stairs and toward the kitchen, following the smell of pancakes and bacon I had often missed waking up to while on the road. Despite my hangover, I got excited by the heavenly scent filling the house. I picked up my pace, but stopped dead in my tracks as I started rounding the corner to the kitchen, fairly certain I had just heard Serena's voice.

Uh-oh. So she did *stay.*

"You sure your brother ain't gay?" she asked with a chuckle, making my sister laugh.

Shit, I missed that kid. And Serena's question meant that nothing had happened the night before, right?

"I'm *pretty* sure his history with women proves otherwise," Lyric laughed, causing a smirk to spread across my face, which was quickly wiped off again. "Then again, maybe his last girlfriend made him swear off women. It's been years, and it's not like I can be sure about what, or whom, he's doing when they're on tour. I mean, Trent talks, but it seems like they usually try to stay out of each other's pants."

I groaned silently. *Oh, that wording...* That wasn't anything I wanted to think about, especially not early in the morning when I wasn't sure where my dick had or hadn't ended up the night before.

"So... What about the girl he was seeing?"

Serena's words clearly were my cue to make myself known. I hadn't told her all about Rayven, and it definitely wasn't Lyric's place to tell, either.

"Goooooood morrrrrrning," I said, slowly stepping into the kitchen and placing a little kiss on my sister's hair. "Haven't seen you in ages."

"Ugh... You smell like monkey ass," she groaned, her scrunched up nose making her look a lot cuter than her words made her sound.

What a greeting...

"You *look* like monkey ass," I replied with a smirk, stealing a piece of her bacon, ignoring Serena's presence. If I couldn't remember inviting her to stay, for the night *and* for breakfast, it meant it never happened – at least in dick-speak. When I really wanted to, I could be fluent in that... not that Serena deserved it.

"Which means, since we're twins, you look *and* smell like monkey ass," Lyric chuckled, seemingly not realizing her small, but most certainly not insignificant mistake.

"We're not identical, Lyric." I laughed. "Otherwise, you'd have a dick."

She seemed to think about it for a moment. "Orrrr you'd be bleeding every month," she retorted, cocking an eyebrow. I had to admit that was a good one.

"Gee, thanks, asshat," I grimaced, loading a plate with food and pouring a cup of coffee.

"Want some ketchup with that bacon?" Serena chimed in, smirking as she held up the bottle.

"You. Are. Evil." I pointed my fork back and forth at each of them. "Both of you." I shook my head, no longer able to ignore Serena. "Why are you still here?"

"Owen, that's not a nice thing to ask." Lyric frowned around a mouthful of pancake.

"Because I slept with you," Serena replied, shrugging, not even batting an eye.

I wasn't sure you could actually feel it when all the color drained from your face, but if you could, I was sure what I felt now was it. I just waited for the floor to get up and hit me in the face.

"You, uhm... In what sense?" I asked reluctantly, putting my plate down on the counter and plopping down on one of the barstools. Hadn't she just asked Lyric to confirm my sexuality?

Maybe that wasn't about rejecting her at all, but some twisted inquiry about whatever position we ended up in last night... Fuck a duck!

"Do you need me to give you 'the talk'?" my sister all but giggled. "Or how about a couple of synonyms? Having sex, intercourse, fun between the sheets, fucking, knob polishing, doing the deed, dancing the horizontal mambo, banging, bagging someone, hitting it, being carnal, mating, the opposite of abstaining..."

I held my hand up. "As curious as I am about how long you can keep that up, Lyric, I don't think I want you to keep going long enough to start telling me where, or from whom, you've picked up each and every one of those because, honestly, that's where I'm glad there's no such thing as unlimited twin telepathy," I said dryly before she could say more things I never wanted to hear coming from her mouth. Ever.

"My turn!" Serena chuckled.

I threw her a look. Was she seriously going to continue Lyric's list? Not that I wasn't intrigued about how much she could add to it, but that didn't, by any means, imply that I wasn't endlessly relieved by the turn the conversation was taking.

"Slumbering, hibernating, catnapping – or regular napping – dozing, resting, complying to the sandman, snoozing, reposing, dreaming, being unconscious, in an almost coma, sack time, going to la-la land, lethargy, energy-saving mode, recharging your battery, uhm... not being awake..."

"Okay, okay. I get it." I chuckled, holding up my hands. "Maybe I should let the two of you write our next songs. You know, *lyrics*, *serena*des, walking thesauruses..."

"Well, that was one hell of a mood swing," Lyric smirked, shaking her head, as if trying to cover up the fact that she kept looking back and forth between Serena and me.

Nice try. Not.

"He's horrified of sleeping with me... *pardon*, of *fucking* me," Serena threw in before I could begin to explain anything, not that I would have voluntarily done so.

"You're horrified of sex?" Lyric frowned, failing to keep the amusement out of her voice. "Do you need 'the talk' after all? Or does she have a monster 'gina?"

"Oh, we didn't even get to the point where he'd have seen my non-monster 'gina," Serena chuckled.

I really hoped these two wouldn't become friends. I didn't want to have to explain to every media outlet out there why my body was covered in dick-shaped tattoos.

"So we, uh... we didn't?" I cleared my throat, awkwardly rubbing my neck. Yup, that promise to myself would have *really* come in handy, had I made it... and actually managed to *keep* it.

"No, Owen, we didn't," Serena answered matter-of-factly, turning to face me. "You'd made yourself perfectly clear when you were only half-drunk... so I wasn't going to force myself on you when you were beyond drunk. There would've been absolutely no consensus, and I wasn't going to all but roofie you."

"Wow, that was...," I started, but was at a loss for words. I hadn't been expecting anything other than a simple yes or no, and most definitely not such an elaborate, defensive-sounding explanation of why.

"Intense?" Lyric offered, obviously just as stunned by Serena's reply as I was.

Twin telepathy might not always be a thing, but I could tell that, right then, it was working perfectly fine in that my twin sister also wondered if something had happened to Serena in the past, something that prompted her to go down the roofie road – or if it had just been her wonderfully wicked, infinitely twisted sense of humor.

Curiosity and friendship aside, I wasn't going to ask her right then and there if anybody had ever tried to force themselves on her. It seemed to be a topic for another day, unless she was the one to come forward with more information without having to be asked. Knowing her, she would've just gone ahead and shrugged questions off anyway. We were way too similar in that regard.

"And just so y'all know," I said to break the silence, trying to avoid awkwardness as I popped a piece of bacon into my mouth, "I'm not scared of sex. I love sex. Sex is awesome. The more the merrier, but–"

"But you're as emotionally unavailable as a rock," Serena finished, shaking her head in amusement. "I was only trying to add some benefits to this friendship, not to drag you to Vegas to put a ring on it!"

"And as soon as I would've rocked your world... or, rather, your body... you would've become as clingy as Saran Wrap."

"Uh, excuse you. I'm sure it would've been the other way around." She chuckled. "But no, despite having been as hard as a rock, Mr. Sappy-Soup didn't want to ruin our friendship."

"Okay, gross," Lyric grimaced. "As fun as this was in the beginning, I really don't want to hear anything that could even remotely be considered detail about my brother's dick. The fact he even has one is as much detail as I need."

"You should be more bothered if it were missing, but I gotta get going anyway." Serena laughed, hopping off her stool and grabbing a set of keys from the counter. "I have some sketches to finish before opening."

"Hey, Serena?" I asked as she was about to leave the room, looking at her through my lashes and putting on the most charming, boyish smile I could muster. "Will you still give me proper tattoos? No... dick rockets or shit-shaped blobs?"

"Depends on your reaction the next time I'm looking for a lay." She smirked before shaking her head. "I take pride in my art, Owen. Your buttheadedness doesn't change shit about that."

Chapter 9

"**S**o... *What's up with you* and Sir-rain-ah?" Lyric asked as she paraded into my room, uninvited, and fell onto my bed. The weird way she enunciated Serena's name made me raise an eyebrow in question. "Don't give me that look, Ow. When a girl walks into the kitchen in the morning, clearly having spent the night, there are questions. You never bring anyone home. Or maybe you do, but they never spend the night, sneak out unnoticed..."

"I thought it was clear that nothing happened." I frowned, starting to unpack the suitcase I hadn't touched since getting home.

"Oh, puh-lease. It's not like you need to attach a flag to your dick every time you've gotten laid. I'm just..."

"Just what?"

"Curious, I suppose." Lyric shrugged, getting more comfortable. "Did you bring me anything?"

"From my non-night night with Serena? Like what? A stencil?"

"Smartass," she chuckled, throwing a pillow at the back of my head, the smile still audible in her voice when she continued. "From wherever you went last. You always bring me something."

"As if you don't get your daily updates on where we are." I smirked, digging through my suitcase in an attempt to find the little bag from the gift shop.

"I don't know what you're talking about," she lied... badly.

"Sorry, Lyric. I didn't bring you anything."

"Liar." She got up and walked over to where I stood. "Is it a puppy?"

"Hey, I just answered one lie with another." I laughed, watching as she stuck her hand into my luggage, obviously trying to find whatever she thought I had brought her. "But there's nothing alive hiding in my bag, L."

"So... It's a dead kitty then?"

I chuckled, shaking my head. "You need a therapist." Guess I could've ended up with someone a lot worse to grow up with.

"There's a dead therapist in your bag?" she gasped playfully, going through my things.

I frowned after watching her for a moment. "You sure you wanna do that? You may be touching sharticles."

"As if," she scoffed. "Mom raised you too well to put shorts full of shit into a bag. Even *you* aren't that gross."

"You don't know what life on the road does to a person." I sighed dramatically, knowing full well she wasn't buying it. "It's not like we have a washer on the bus. Or Mom close by. Which would be kinda the same thing."

"So it'd be okay for *Mom* to get your sharticles on her hands, but not me?" she chuckled, pulling out the small black organza bag from between my clothes. "Is this it?"

"I just figured *you'd* be the one who'd have a problem with it."

She chuckled. "Ha! I've been putting up with your shit for as long as I can remember. You probably shat all over me in the womb."

"I'm... I'm not sure that's how that works." I frowned again. Being around her for an extended period of time would probably end up giving me wrinkles.

Was that how it worked? I mean, I knew where babies came from and how they were made – especially how they were made because I had plenty of pleasurable practice – but did babies take actual shits? And what happened to the turds? It wasn't like they could just flush. Maybe that was why a woman's water broke. Their fetus decided it was time to stop swimming in shit, so they pulled the plug.

Fetus Feces... Too bad our band already has a name.

"Gross," I mumbled, grimacing, wondering how my mind could have wandered off that far. *Downside of creative minds, eh?* Maybe that meant being home would give me not only the time, but also the muse to write a few more of the new songs our producer was after.

"Earth to Owen? Where did you just go?" Lyric asked, waving a hand in front of my face. People really needed to stop doing that.

"I, uh... Nowhere. Sorry." *Aside from basically literally down the gutter, all the way to the sewer.*

"So... Is this mine?" she asked with the sweetest smile on her face. She probably missed traveling more than she let on, and the little knickknacks from the road allowed her, to some extent, to travel along with me and the boys.

"Well, so far, it's been mine, but yeah, you can have it." I grinned, shrugging, pretending I had just decided it should be hers. "Tough shit if you don't like it."

"Thankies," she beamed, hopping back to the bed and sitting down cross-legged, looking as excited as a little kid on Christmas morning. Sometimes it was hard to believe we were the same age – plus or minus a few minutes, depending on whose age you were comparing to whose.

"You don't even know what it is yet. You might hate it."

"Not going by your usual standards. Besides, the shape of the bag's sorta telling, so putting tissue paper in with it was kinda useless," she chuckled, unwrapping her little gift.

"That was the store, not me. I don't do... cute."

"Oh, sure you do," she retorted, still chuckling, holding up the small plastic snow globe dangling from a keychain. "It's beautiful." She smiled, watching the light shine off the little sparkles swimming through the liquid surrounding a black bird.

"There's a big souvenir one from the town somewhere in my other bag, too, but when I saw that one..." I trailed off, seeing the look she gave me.

She already knows.

"It made you think of her. I get it." She nodded, biting her lip. "But you know, Owen, sometimes you just gotta let go. It's been years. Don't get me wrong. You're not the only one missing her. What makes you think she'll ever come back, though? That you'll actually hear from her again? It's not like she's been dropping in and out. She's just... *gone.* No notes, no letters, no emails or texts, no fuckin' Facebook requests. Nothing."

"I know, L," I sighed, rubbing my neck a bit. "I just haven't been able to let go. Believe me, I've tried. Moving on is far from easy."

"Guess you haven't found the right distraction yet," Lyric replied, sadness evident in her voice.

"I've found plenty of *distraction*," I scoffed with a humorless laugh. The problem was that I wasn't longing for distraction, but for love. For *her.* For the love of someone who might have, true to my sister's words, been gone for good. For all we knew, her name could have been carved into a tombstone on some graveyard far away, while I waited for her to come back home to me.

"Sorry," she grimaced, climbing off my bed again.

"I didn't mean to make this... sullen. I love the gift. I really do. I can't wait to see the big one." She smiled softly, stepping closer and tightly wrapping her arms around me.

"I'm working on it," I mumbled into her hair as I returned the hug.

"When it's true love, I guess a heart doesn't just break. It shatters," she whispered, slowly pulling away.

"If you're not careful with what you say, your words just may end up in my next song," I replied in an attempt to lighten the mood.

"Just, you know, give me a special section in the acknowledgments, and we're good."

First Serena, now her.

"You already got my keyboarder. Now you want a whole section in the next album's acknowledgments? Greedy much?" I asked jokingly, prompting her to give me the finger as she walked out of my room, innocently voicing everyone's favorite lie.

"I have no idea what you're talking about, Ow."

Chapter 10

Being home always meant doing quite a bit of press. People knew you and were somewhat proud you were "theirs". They thought you were comfortable enough on home turf to spill a little more information than elsewhere, and management was usually on your ass not to lay low while you weren't touring. To them, not touring apparently equaled the principle of *out of sight, out of mind*, although it obviously didn't mean people would just stop listening to your music. I, for one, never stopped listening to an artist's or a band's music just because I couldn't see them perform live. I mean, c'mon. Some of the greatest music had been produced before I'd ever been born. Had being dead made Kurt Cobain's music any less awesome? Had The Clash's music lost its rock because they weren't around to perform live anymore? Had people stopped listening to Michael Jackson because they could no longer see him grab his crotch on stage? No? Didn't think so.

Contrary to what many people may think, not being on the road wasn't equal to having time off, although it was when we got to spend most of our time with family and friends, of course. We had to continue writing songs, doing press interviews, photoshoots, and miscellaneous other appearances.

Usually, with the exception of the very few bad experiences we had, the boys and I loved every second of it with every fiber of our beings. We were grateful we got to do what we loved while being paid for it. It was something we had never taken for granted; hopefully, that would never change.

We had waited for our chance, more than ready when opportunity presented itself, and each one of us was well aware that not everyone who loved doing music got their moment to shine as brightly as they should. That was also the reason we hadn't turned down appearing on one of the local stations' evening shows, even though their interviewer was known to ask questions that made their guests more than uncomfortable.

"Ready to be asked about your lack of love life?" Jimmy asked half-jokingly. I put a halt to my pacing only long enough to glare at him.

"Am I ever?" I grumbled, moving my head from side to side, popping my neck. "But I'm even less ready to have Trent asked about his."

"*Burrr-urrr-urn!*" Jimmy laughed, looking over at Trent.

"I didn't bring your sister's panties, so don't get yours into a twist," Trent replied, holding up his hands in defense.

In any other situation, his words would have probably prompted some witty remark in response, or a fist to his nose, but I felt as though I should save all my energy, my wit and charm, for Nicole Morningstar, who had once been tagged as "the most devilish interviewer you never want to have the pleasure to sit across from." Personally, I had never thought her broadcast to be *that* bad, but I also hadn't set foot in her studio, let alone run into her backstage... yet. Maybe evil lurked just around the corner, ready to plunge its fangs into us to steal our souls.

Overdramatic much, Owen?

Evidently, I was nowhere near having reached immunity to stage fright.

"Was that a confession?" It was all I could muster as I raised an eyebrow at one of my best friends. I could feel all eyes on us – and by *all*, I didn't only mean those of the other guys, but also the pair belonging to the leggy blonde who had just walked through the door.

Nicole Morningstar.

"Good thing you're about to go on. I can figure things out for you." She smiled so sweetly, it was almost sickening. Of course, that may have been thanks to my nervousness.

"No reason to. We can figure out our own shit." Trent shook his head, making her laugh.

"We'll see about that." She nodded, her voice oozing amusement as she motioned for us to follow her to the stage door. "As you should all be aware, this will be a live show. One of our production assistants will let you know when to come in. There will be a total of two short commercial breaks. Questions?"

"We already got briefed," Jimmy commented, making Nicole roll her eyes.

"I like to make sure things go according to plan myself. The show isn't what it is because things just *happen*," she responded. I wasn't sure if she was annoyed or shocked that one of us had the nerve to imply what she was doing was unnecessary.

After that, things seemed to happen pretty fast. A girl wearing glasses, whose name tag read "Maggy", her name subtitled by the word "intern", made sure we waited for our cue to enter. I was sure Jimmy was more than just a little tempted to strip out of his clothes and run across the stage naked. Luckily for Maggy, and her internship, he behaved. We all did, patiently waiting for Nicole to announce us before entering the camera-filled part of the studio, hearing applause and whistling from the, presumably, mainly female audience who had filled the seats to see us. Or, well, *maybe* Nicole... though I highly doubted it.

"Well, well. What a warm welcome for some SoCal locals!" Nicole said with a smile big enough to make me wonder what dentist she was seeing. Somehow, her demeanor and accentuation reminded me of *Effie Trinket*.

The same smile still plastered in place, she turned from looking directly into the camera to face us when one of the production assistants gave her a sign that camera views were being switched. Watching television people work never grew old. "It is a great pleasure to have you here, boys. I promise, we'll keep things juicy!"

"The juiciest thing I've seen all day's been your ass when you left us gawking after you," Chuck replied, earning the first round of snickers from the audience.

Well played.

"You're making me blush," Nicole giggled, pulling up a shoulder and touching her cheek, which hadn't reddened at all, as if she were attempting to pose for a wanna-be pinup shoot.

I wasn't going to turn into her biggest fan anytime soon. Sure, she was just doing her job, which contributed to us getting to do ours, but damn. I had never seen anybody so fake. I couldn't help but wonder why people tuned in to her show. Couldn't have been because of her wit and charm.

"So, first and foremost, we've been wondering, and there's been much speculation online, why do you call yourselves The Knuggets?" Nicole flipped her hair over her shoulder, as if that were going to get her a better answer than not whipping her hair like a horse in heat. At least her "first and foremost" question didn't revolve around anyone's bedroom stories, though.

"Did she just say *Knuggets*?" Jimmy asked, his voice an octave or two higher than usual, his whole body starting to shake with laughter. He had always been the tallest, lankiest one of us, and he had the tendency to look like a giant, out-of-control praying mantis when he cracked up. Or like one of the hyenas from that Disney movie with the lions, which we hadn't been allowed to watch more than once as kids because it always made Lyric cry. The memory made me smile to myself.

"What the fuck's a Knugget s'pposed to be?" Jake frowned.

I was glad he pulled me back out of my reverie before our interviewer could try to sink her claws into my thoughts.

"That's exactly what we'd like to know. How about you shed some light on that for us?" the vulture inquired, batting her lashes. Knowing what reaction she hoped to get, I figured I'd make things as easy as possible on all of us and just take the bait.

"How about I give you that talk backstage, Nikki? It's okay to call you Nikki, right? Just with... not that much actual *talking* involved?" I asked suggestively, earning an *ooooooh* from the audience. Looking at her with a cocked brow, I was happy to see how flustered our interviewer actually appeared.

Mission accomplished.

That kind of behavior was expected from us. If it meant we'd get to keep doing what we loved, we were happy to deliver, even if it made us uneasy at times. I mean, let's face it. It was easy marketing... a little flirt, the occasional wink, an otherwise inappropriate word here and there. Not everyone was just in it for the music. A probably rather considerable part of our rising success were our faces and bodies, not just our voices and talents – especially where younger audiences, and fans of the opposite gender, were concerned.

Watching Nicole fumble with her papers for a moment, Jake decided to put her out of her misery. "It's The C-Nuggets. Just the way it's spelled," he chuckled, using the family-friendly abbreviation of our band's name, which had misled her to believe we were called The Knuggets.

Bummer.

"So, which one of you likes chicken nuggets enough to name the band after them?" she asked, back to sounding all chipper in the blink of an eye, obviously thinking she had just cracked the case.

Poor naïve little interviewer.

That moment would probably be eternalized by the internet's finest memes. I could already see the corresponding GIF before my eyes – her entirely overly enthusiastic self, all smiles, asking us about shredded chicken babies, followed by all five of us howling with laughter, fading into a picture of her falling face. Surely she'd consider becoming a reporter for a newspaper or a smut-clippings writer for a magazine after this. The latter would probably be right down her alley.

From behind one of the cameras, I saw the producer signaling to her, most likely asking if she needed some sort of emergency intermission, an unplanned commercial break to compose herself.

She cleared her throat. "So, uhm... If not chicken, what's the 'c' for? I assume you're not the Cute-Nuggets, a spiced-up version of cutie-pies?"

Smooth. Real smooth, I thought, just about to say something, but Jimmy beat me to it.

"Cunt," he simply replied, visibly trying his hardest to keep a straight face.

Clearly taken aback, Nicole sat up a bit straighter, clearing her throat again. "I am not sure that was called for or appropriate on any level imaginable. Why are you calling me a...?" It looked like it suddenly dawned on her. She seemed embarrassed, but I honestly wasn't sure if it was *because* of us or *for* us. "Oh, right. So you're... you're The *Cunt*-Nuggets?"

Maybe she wasn't quite as bad as people always made her out to be, or as bad as I had already started to think she was, but simply too sure of herself and coming across as somewhat of a... fake bitch. And a *lottle*, not just a little, fake, as earlier observations had shown. But when you caught her off guard, like we apparently just had – she seemed to not be familiar with the concept of Google; otherwise, she could have figured out what the "c" stood for prior to the interview – she was actually pretty fun to watch. At least if, like me, you found amusement in the awkwardness of others.

"Yes, ma'am." Chuck smiled proudly, as if he were talking about his not-yet-existent firstborn and not one of the English language's most frowned upon words.

Shit, I really love these guys.

"How did that name come to be? Surely you didn't just wake up one day and call yourselves The... C-Nuggets," she said after a moment, unwilling to use the band's full name.

"The Invalids and Fetus Feces had been up for discussion, but

The Cunt-Nuggets won by a long shot," I smirked jokingly, even though those options had only circulated through *my* mind, never really standing a chance of becoming our name.

"His sister came up with it," Trent threw in. I couldn't keep myself from giving him a look. Of course, Trenton would be the first one to point that one out.

"Is that so?" Nicole asked, obviously smelling blood. Trent himself was the only one to blame for that, so I sure as hell wasn't going to help him get out of it.

"Yeah... She spent some time in Europe back in high school, and a friend of hers from the UK used that terminology a lot. Once she got back home, they were video chatting one day. Apparently, we were a little too loud and vulgar in the background, so her friend said, 'Can't those cunt nuggets shut their fuckin' cakeholes?'" Trent explained. "Afterward, Lyric, Owen's sister, kept calling us that, so we figured we may as well go with. It's officially been our name ever since."

"And this Lyric you are referring to... She's your girlfriend?" Nicole asked sweetly, tilting her head to the side in that popular puppy-dog look that had probably gotten her one too many answers in the past.

"She's his sister." Trent replied half-assedly, nodding his head toward me. "His twin, actually."

"I see." She nodded slowly, her eyes wandering to me. "And you're okay with that?"

"Tough question." I shrugged, taking a deep breath and running a hand through my hair, trying to look like I was sincerely giving my answer a lot of thought. "I didn't have much of a choice. I mean, sure, I could have probably eaten her while we were still in the womb, but once we were out, we were out, and I was stuck with her. I once tried talking Mom into leaving her at the grocery store, but our mother wasn't all too happy with the suggestion, saying Lyric didn't look enough like an eggplant to be left with the rest of the vegetables. All that got me was a slap to the back of the head, that little gnome still with us on the way back home, so..."

"I, uh... I meant Trent and your sister dating," she said amusedly. "I mean, that's what you were bickering about backstage, wasn't it?"

"I wasn't aware we were *bickering*," I chuckled, glancing at Trent. "You got a beef, man?"

"Nah." Trent smirked, shaking his head. "Unless you're talking about dinner. Wouldn't mind a taco or two."

"So there's nothing going on between you and your frontman's little sister? I'd assume that would cause quite a bit of... friction."

"Between! The! Sheets!" Chuck threw in, probably to defuse the situation a little, making the audience laugh.

"Can that be considered confirmation?" Nicole asked, a little too excitedly.

"Depends... Can porn be considered PG?" Chuck asked, causing the studio guests to laugh once again.

"Right," she mumbled, clearing her throat a little before attempting a different approach. "That new song you will be presenting to us in just a few short moments..." She had to pause until the applause died down. "Is it safe to assume that you, Trent, wrote it for Lyric?"

"Negative," Trent answered, shaking his head. "That song was all Owen."

"Is that so?" she asked curiously, directing her attention to me, which, to be honest, made me more than just a little uncomfortable. Trent's words could only lead to one line of questioning. One I loved to avoid like the plague.

"Well... I do the vocals, so a lot of the songs have either been written or co-written by me. *Lyrics* and I just kinda go together. It's like I was born with them."

"I see that all of you like to play with words," she said, sounding anything but happy about not getting the answers she had hoped for. Tough luck. None of us minded answering questions related to our music or the band, but we all liked keeping some aspects of our lives private. "But are you really trying to tell me the lyrics to 'My Refrain', one of the new songs on your upcoming album, are a pure work of fiction? No... real-life story behind the words? No specific experience you drew inspiration from?"

"We all draw inspiration from something." I shook my head, biting my lip for a moment. "Most of the time, it's everyday things. Emotions, feelings. Without them, our stories – our songs – would be meaningless and convey nothing but a big fat zero to the listener. So yes, I did draw inspiration from real life, from true emotion, as we all do when we use a creative outlet. But how much of it is actually based on a story of my life, and how much of it is fiction, as you've put it?"

I smirked. "That's for me to know and for you to, well, not."

"I see." She nodded with a small frown, regarding me, as if she were debating asking another question.

Suddenly, she plastered her trademark smile back onto her face as she looked at the camera. "We will be right back after a short commercial break. When we come back, The C-Nuggets will give us an exclusive first look, or I should say listen, of their new album! Stay tuned. You won't want to miss this!"

———◆———

"They're probably showing some kinda tampon commercial right about now," Jimmy laughed as we walked toward our instruments, earning a slap on the back of his head from Jake. "Duuuude, what was that for?"

"Tampons," Jake scoffed, shaking his head.

"Go get ready to use your hands instead of your mouth... not that I ever thought I'd say that," Jimmy chuckled, picking up his guitar. "Listen, most of the people watching are probably chicks. Fifty bucks says every commercial is tampons and pregnancy tests while we're on."

"You owe me fifty," Jake concluded, popping his fingers in preparation.

"Ready in three, two...," some guy with a clipboard announced, holding up one finger, then pointing to us, stopping Jimmy from making yet another remark about female hygiene products.

Right on cue, Trent started pushing down the keys of the keyboard, which served as our on-the-road piano for smaller shows. The song's intro echoed off the studio's walls, met by excited cheering from the crowd. The other guys joined in, creating the bittersweet melody that served as the acoustic backdrop for our newest hard rock ballad. The album wouldn't be out for another couple weeks, but nothing caused as much anticipation as a sneak peek. When timed right, early exposure was a great, if not the best, promotion.

Wrapping my hands around the microphone on the stand in front of me, I closed my eyes and took a deep breath, soaking up every nuance of the music, ignoring the spotlight I stood in. As soon as the boys started on the right bar, I let the words slip out of my mouth, putting my heart and soul into every syllable, emotionally draining myself.

My heart, it didn't break when you left.
True love, it left it shattered.
[shattered, shattered]
It feels like the greatest theft
'cause you're all that ever mattered.
[mattered, mattered]

I believe in music, not in fairy tales.
In your world, it snows.
In mine, it hails.
What would I have achieved
If I'd just believed?

[Belie-ieved]

You spread your wings,
You flew away,
[ah, buh-bye]
No, I'm not okay.
[oh-kay-ay]
Like a knife, it stings.
[every day]

My heart, it didn't break when you left.
True love, it left it shattered.
[shattered, shattered]
It feels like the greatest theft
'cause you're all that ever mattered.
[mattered, mattered]

On, I should move.
[move on]
My heart, my brain, they disapprove.
[disapprove]
Like a glass slipper, you left me behind.
Help! I can't get you out of my mind.
[always on my mind]

What if you're my refrain
And I can't love again?
If you're truly the only one who fits the shoe,
Say who can replace you?
[say who]

My heart, it didn't break when you left.
True love, it left it shattered.
[shattered, shattered]
It feels like the greatest theft
'cause you're all that ever mattered.
[mattered, mattered]

Why, if you're the only Cinderella,
Am I not your Prince Charming fella?
You set the beat of my heart,
No chance to restart.

You've flown away.
I wish you'd stayed.
[stayed away]
Please, come back.
Make it all less black.
Be my light again,
My everlasting refrain.

[come back again]

The moment the music faded out, it was evident we had won over the audience. Judging by the noise they made, they thoroughly enjoyed the music, the sound... and maybe even the lyrics had spoken to them. Trying to catch my breath – not because it had been a physically exhausting performance, but because I had put myself out there a lot more than I usually did – I welcomed the second commercial break, along with the cold bottle of water someone handed me.

"Dude, that was sick." Chuck smiled as he walked out from behind his drum set, tossing his sticks into the audience, which were followed by a couple guitar picks from the other guys. "Honestly, I didn't think we could pull it off live, with the background vocals being so..."

"Soft?" Trent threw in, seeming amused, but just as hyped as the rest of us. Performing on stage was a high like no other.

"Well, yeah, kinda. Sorta cheesy wording, considering the music we've been pairing it with," Chuck laughed as we sat back on the sofas in front of Nicole.

⎯⎯•◆•⎯⎯

"Didn't I tell you that would be a performance you wouldn't want to miss?" Nicole asked the audience, her toothpaste-commercial smile frozen in place. "I'd say that sure as hell was a promise I kept!"

Luckily, the audience agreed, their cheers rocking the room.

However, I wasn't entirely sure whether I should be looking forward to or dreading the little question and answer session planned for our last few minutes on air. While people attending such events could usually be considered friendly fans, you never knew if a crazy one hid among them... and you certainly never knew just how personal their questions would be. Maybe being in the industry made me a little... socially paranoid?

"Y'all were lucky enough to get tickets to today's show," Nicole continued. "Now you'll get even luckier and have the chance to ask these boys some questions. Our Maggy, the girl in blue, will be walking around with the microphone. Just raise your hand if you have a question you would like to ask, and we'll try to give as many of you as possible the opportunity to get some answers!"

Audience member after audience member got handed the microphone. Thanks to there not being much of it to begin with, time seemed to fly. To be fair, I was quite surprised at how clean people kept their questions – the majority of them hadn't made inquiries about anything below the belt. They'd stayed classy and hadn't crossed any lines. Only one young woman had actually, rather nervously, brought herself to ask if she could have my baby. A lot of celebrities may have been used to questions like that, but being asked directly was a first for me. Hoping it wouldn't mark me as an arrogant asshole, I didn't know any better way to answer than with humor. I actually promised her I would let her know "once I've decided to put my little swimmers up for grabs as part of charity." I could only hope that statement wouldn't haunt me for the rest of our career.

"To wrap things up, I just have to try once again." Nicole smiled, looking straight at me. "That song... Whom have you written it for? It was so full of feeling..."

Of course she would have to ask the question I had mentally thanked the whole audience for not asking. Of course she couldn't just let it go. Of course she had to push. And *of course* I couldn't just flip her off and storm off stage during a live show, even if I felt like it. Instead, I regarded her for a moment, sorting out my words, promising myself I would think back to that exact moment whenever I felt like I just wasn't cut out for adulting.

"That's our job, though, isn't it?" I answered calmly. "I mean... The moment music stops conveying emotion will be the moment we can start listening to grey noise instead. It will be the moment music has died."

Chapter 11

"**D**uuuuuude, that was some sick* poetic shit in there!" Jimmy beamed on the way home, making it sound like I had just quoted Emily Dickinson rather than expressed my general opinion of music when asked about... matters of the heart, for the lack of better words.

"What I don't get, though," Jake threw in from the back seat, "is why you didn't just spill the beans."

"Because it's nobody's fuckin' business," I sighed, staring up at the red light and tapping my fingers against the steering wheel, impatiently waiting for it to turn green so I could get us all home – another plus of not being too far away. Only traveling short distances meant it was easier to be evasive, even when it was your best friends who were asking one too many questions.

"The whole thing was live on television, Owen." I looked in the rearview mirror to see Jake shaking his head. "It will most likely end up online – the show's page, YouTube, the little fan page that's been set up. Shared all over social media, basically. If you're still hung up on her enough to create this kind of – sorry for the cheese – beautiful shit, then why not try to use those outlets to your advantage?"

"You mean... just put it all out there? Some sort of a search for her?" I asked dubiously, starting to drive again when the light changed. "I'm not sure that'd be a smart idea."

"Nah, you're right." Trent shook his head, the hint of sarcasm in his voice not going unnoticed. "It wouldn't be smart. It'd be fuckin' *brilliant!*"

"I think it'd just make the waiting worse. The waiting that I've done enough of and am trying to stop doing, remember? Trying to let go and all that shit. Isn't that what this whole album's supposed to be about? A way to move on?"

"Yeah, well... Maybe, maybe not. It doesn't have to be," Jake replied. I let out a frustrated little sigh, which faded into a rather humorless, quiet chuckle. "What's funny?"

"The fact that all of you tried your damnedest to get me to *stop* hoping, and now... Now you're making it sound like hope would be the best thing to have. Like putting myself out there, all but publicly begging her to come back, will actually make someone drop her off on our back porch."

"Well, you did say tha–" Jimmy started, but I cut him off, slapping his chest with the back of my hand before he could share my drunken antics with the rest of the guys. No matter how much I trusted each and every one of them, I didn't need to have them psychoanalyze my stories about Rayven. Things were messed up enough without my every word being scrutinized.

"That whole reverse psychology stuff y'all are trying to pull? It's gonna do jack shit. If she hears the songs and feels like they're about her, she can come back and be my fucking guest of honor, but I'm not gonna put her name all over the place."

"We decided to call the album *Rayvenous*, man, remember?" Jimmy threw in with an almost nervous-sounding laugh. "With a 'y'. The artwork's done. The name's been announced. You can't decide you want to pull all obvious traces of her now."

"I'm not... Shit! Would you just let me drive before we all end up looking like crushed ice," I grumbled, trying to stay somewhat focused on the road, despite my mind running on overdrive. Were they being serious about wanting me to basically give her a shout-out in the hopes she was watching, listening? Or were they just being my non-biological shitheaded brothers, giving me royal crap, waiting for me to snap?

Was she still somewhere out there, waiting for a clear sign that she'd be welcomed back?

"If she's listening, she'll know," I said quietly as I pulled into Chuck's driveway to drop him off.

"Can't hurt to give things a little push or a soft nudge here and there, though." Chuck smirked as he climbed out. "Today was great, guys! Nothing like the thrill of performing a song on stage for the first time. Here's to the ones to follow!"

After Chuck, I drove the remaining guys home. Only Jimmy decided to linger in the car a little longer than necessary, prompting me to kill the engine. Rolling my eyes, I let my head fall back against the headrest, taking a deep breath, bracing myself for whatever he had to say.

When he still hadn't spoken after what felt like an eternity, I glanced at him slowly. The way he regarded me was almost creepy, like a clown pondering his next step... to either go for the kill or only be a creep?

"C'mon, James. Spill it," I sighed.

It wasn't like I was dying to hear his thoughts on the whole dilemma once again, but the longer he looked at me without saying shit, the more anxious I grew. Constantly being judged for something you didn't know how to control didn't exactly make moments of silent staring seem like a tea party.

"Why is it so hard for you to let go?"

"I don't know, man," I replied with another sigh, gripping the steering wheel a little harder, although we weren't going anywhere. "Don't you think I'd have taken it if I'd found a magic way out?"

"You never had any problems moving on from your past girlfriends. Ex-lovers. Onesies and serial deed doers."

"Dude, I get it."

"So?" James prompted.

I rolled my eyes. Was he really expecting an answer different from those he had received the other nine billion times he had asked?

"Yeah, well, much like penguins and pigeons, ravens mate for life," I said dryly, unable to come up with a better answer. To be fair, I was aware of the level of shit it may have contained, but it was a reply nonetheless. Judging by the corners of Jimmy's lips tugging up, he must have somewhat approved of it more than of a response consisting of an eye roll or an exasperated sigh instead of words.

"Yeah, but she's a person," he responded amusedly and a little absentmindedly, probably planning on asking the World Wide Web about the mating rituals of black birds.

"You sure?"

All things considered, it really was only half a question. She had appeared out of nowhere, claiming to have sprung from a snow globe-like, unearthly world, then disappeared just as fast as she had stepped – or, rather, fallen – into my life, our lives, and stolen my heart.

"Well... Does she have a belly button?" Jimmy asked.

I couldn't help but laugh, making him look at me like he was finally convinced I had bid the last piece of my sanity goodbye. And I just might have.

"I asked her the same thing once," I said through my laughter, albeit unable to keep the sadness out of my voice.

"And?"

"She hated it."

"Does she, though?"

"Yeah..." I nodded slowly, rubbing my face as flashes of her naked body passed behind my eyes. I could confirm she most certainly did have a belly button because I had checked. She was – or had been – as anatomically correct as they came.

"Maybe it's artificial," Jimmy offered with a smirk, his mission of putting me in a better mood not failing, even if I was still nowhere near ready to erase her from my mind.

"An artificial navel? Dude, you high?" I smirked back, narrowing my eyes, shooting him a *what the fuck* look. "If so, you forgot to share."

"You saying a fake belly button would be crazier than that whole story about Snowmania?"

"*Snowden,*" I corrected, biting back another sigh. Would an artificial belly button really have been a more abstract idea than someone having lived inside – and escaped from – a snow globe? Somewhat defeated, I slightly shook my head. "Guess it wouldn't be."

It was hard to admit because realizing, and admitting, just how ridiculous the idea must have sounded to someone not as invested as I was made the distance between us seem even greater, decreasing the probability of her ever returning, ever coming back to me.

"So... Has it been helping?" Jimmy quietly asked after a moment of silence, almost as if afraid his words could break me. Once he realized I had no idea what he was referring to, he continued, specifying his question. "The sappy song writing?"

"Oh." I frowned, running a hand through my hair. I sure as hell wouldn't have called it that. To be fair, the lyrics of the songs included on *Rayvenous* dealt with different topics than most of our previous ones and were less vulgar and a little more... poetic, but I still wouldn't have characterized them as sappy. The kind of music we had paired the words with made sure people wouldn't end up labelling us as soft rockers. We played genuine rock music with strong inclinations toward hard rock and influenced by metal, so there was nothing cotton balled about our sound.

"You're not one for answering questions today, are you?" he chuckled.

"I don't know. I really appreciate that you've all been going along with it, giving me a creative outlet, but... I'd be lying if I said I was any more ready to let go than I was before."

"Figured," he nodded. "You're just a big ol' bowl of sappy soup."

"Jesus fuckin' Christ on a cracker with cheese, Jimmy. Thanks."

"There you go, man. Soup and crackers. What more do you need?"

"Distraction."

Maybe, just maybe, I should have taken Serena up on her offer of making me forget – even if just for a night.

Chapter 12

"**S***ere-eeeh-naaah*," *I said* in a sing-song voice as I walked into her parlor the next evening just a few minutes before closing time, a bottle of booze in hand... which I might or might not have taken a few swigs from on the way over.

Right after dropping Jimmy off the night before, I had successfully talked myself out of choosing distraction over the usual, comfortably established wallowing, but it was also the day I decided it was time to try something new. Or old, considering I hadn't shied away from the occasional random road-shag in the past. What was new, however, was planning to have sex with someone I had known for a while, someone I liked enough to call a friend, someone I had essentially been planning to stay friends with – not to mention I wanted her to continue putting her art on my skin.

Putting it like that actually made me second-guess proposing we enter the stage of friends with benefits. What if it ended up biting us in the rear? After all, it could have turned into a one-time, I-really-don't-want-to-see-your-fucking-face-ever-again kind of thing, ruining our friendship.

Because shit happens.

"Owww-owww-owwwen?" she mimicked my tone, laughing at my greeting as she put her pencil down and looked up from behind the counter.

"What are you up to?" I asked as I stepped closer to sneak a peek, nosey about what she had been working on.

"Just doodling some wanna-dos, letting the creative juices flow." She smiled, looking at me just as curiously as I had been at her. "What brings Mr. Rock Star here this time of day?"

"I was wondering if... the offer still stands?" I smirked, placing the bottle on the counter, as if it were some kind of trade offering.

"The offer? For reduced piercing rates? Tattoo deals? Owen, as much as I like you, I'm not firing the machines back up five minutes before the shop closes, especially not with you on the verge of being tipsy."

"No, I, uh... I meant the offer for some nakey-nakey time." I chuckled, raising an eyebrow. "You have special tattoo deals?"

"For the wanna-dos." She shrugged casually. "It's easier to get stuff *you* really wanna do on people if you're not asking as much as for tattoos *they* really want to begin with."

"Gotcha." I nodded, watching her regard me carefully, her eyes wandering down and back up my body as much as the counter in between us allowed.

"Are you being serious this time, Owen? You've pretty much blue balled me before." Her words made me chuckle. "I don't like being cockblocked by the subject of my shagging plans."

"You don't have balls. Or a cock to block," I said before my snicker subsided and I was left frowning a little. "At least I hope you don't. I mean, I haven't checked... yet."

"Relax," she said, laughing as she shook her head. "I don't. Everything's where, and the way, it's supposed to be."

"That's really good to know. Thanks for the reassurance." I nodded, my eyes not leaving her as she started to shut down the computers. "So...?"

"Will you let me close down first, or do you have a pressing case of jack-in-the-box threatening to make your zipper pop?"

I chuckled. "Yeah... No, I'm good. Has anyone ever told you you had a big mouth?"

"Not before they've had the pleasure of 'nakey-nakey time'." She smirked over her shoulder, probably not entirely unaware of just having gotten us a step closer to the jack-in-the-box phenomenon, as she had put it. "Has it ever crossed your mind that I am just as comfortable in my skin as everyone should be, so I can usually say what I want without feeling like I should hide a moment later?"

"Kudos to you, Serena." I smiled, taking another sip from the bottle. "I like straight forward. It's good."

"Maybe you shouldn't drink too much before you start getting all glum and broody again."

"Duly noted."

"I mean it. I'm not giving you the chance to blue ball me thrice. I have a two strikes rule."

"Isn't it usually a *three* strikes rule?" I asked with what I hoped would come across as a playful pout, my eyes dropping to her lips when she leaned across the counter, stopping no more than an inch short of my face.

"I'm the master of my panties, Owen," Serena whispered, almost sounding a bit wicked, "so I'm the one making the rules. And if I say it's two strikes, it's two strikes."

I wasn't aware of just how close Serena lived to her shop. No wonder it had so often seemed like she actually lived there. Before I watched her lock the doors, I had somewhat been under the impression we would be spreading our germs all over the parlor – which was exactly what she ended up telling me she wanted to avoid, even though the smell of green soap wasn't exactly a turn-off for either one of us. On the contrary. I was sure being in the shop could have made either one of us even more frisky... not that we needed it. At least I assumed that applied to both of us, not just me.

"Must be great living so close to work. Means you don't have to get up too early." I smirked as I followed her up the stairs to her apartment.

"It's not as great as traveling the world. I'm sure you see a shit ton more than most people dream of. I experience very little compared to a lot of people."

"You could do conventions in different parts of the country, or even the world." I shrugged. "Or you could join us on the road for a few stops."

"Calm your tits, hot stuff. Just because we're about to have some adult fun doesn't mean we'll be girlfriending anytime soon. Or ever."

"That's... not what I meant. No offense."

"None taken," she chuckled as she unlocked the door, revealing a small, tidy apartment. "You're kinda touchy when it comes to giving you shit in that department."

"And what department is that?" I asked as I looked at some of the drawings pinned to her living room walls, although I most certainly knew what she had been playing at. "These are amazing."

"Thanks." She smiled, slipping off her boots.

"A department we will no longer be discussing tonight."

"What will we be discussing instead then?" I smirked as she hooked her fingers through the belt loops of my jeans.

"Nothing that requires many words. How about that?" She steered me in what I assumed to be the direction of her bedroom, since we weren't getting any closer to the sofa.

"Mmmh... I think I approve."

I leaned in to capture her lips with mine, not even remotely as appalled by the idea of kissing her, touching her, as I had been when she'd shown up at my parents' place the other night. Not that the location had been the issue, but the soft feel of her lips was much more enjoyable now that I was the initiator, rather than having her practically throwing herself at me while I was in the midst of getting lost in a drunken reverie.

"You sure you're okay with this? A... non-*girlfriending* booty call?" I mumbled against her lips when the back of my legs hit what I believed to be her bed, using her previous wording to describe what we weren't going to be doing.

"I suggested it, remember?" she asked against my skin, her lips wandering to my neck as my hands slipped under her shirt.

"Just checking."

I groaned quietly when she sank her teeth into the spot where my neck and shoulder met. It was a playful bite, but I felt it shoot straight to my groin. Tilting my head to the side to grant her better access, I hoped she'd hit some of my favorite spots. Instead, she pulled away, looking at me as if she were scolding me.

"Just because I have a vagina instead of a dick doesn't mean I can't enjoy a great lay, does it?" She smiled, pulling off my shirt and admiring the artwork on my skin, as if she were laying eyes on it for the first time.

"Who says it's gonna be great?" I chuckled softly, freeing her from her maple-red Henley. My eyes scanned her body, admiring the black lace bra she was wearing, as if she had foreshadowed my visit. Pretty or not, it wasn't meant to stay in place for long, if you asked me, especially with how she had reacted to my making sure she hadn't changed her mind.

I unsnapped it with one hand, sliding it down her arms and carelessly letting it drop to the floor, where it looked even better than on her.

"Here's to hoping it will be." She smirked as she undid my belt. "If it isn't, there simply won't be a repeat performance."

In the matter of seconds, the rest of our clothing was gone, strewn across the floor, crumbled up in heaps. Just like our clothes, our hands and lips were everywhere, all over each other, exploring, feverish, relentless. Impatient, unforgiving, and unashamed. What we were doing wasn't lovemaking to either one of us. We were both trying to satisfy our inner beasts, all rationality lost.

"Shit...," I groaned when I felt her lips wrap around me, my hand disappearing into her hair and balling into a fist, needing to hold on to something. Aside from a few more moaned profanities, that was to be the last word either one of us would speak for a long time.

When she had first propositioned me, I figured she just wanted a casual screw, simple acts of fornication, but not... all-around treatment. I sure as hell wasn't going to complain, though. Everything that followed were pure acts of ecstasy. Before long, I was completely engulfed by her.

One erratic thrust met another, wild moans and sighs of pleasure faded into one another, leaving us insatiable.

At some point during round two, we found a common rhythm, neither one of us in a rush to finish.

Round three left us both drained, a temporary sense of bliss and satisfaction washing over me.

Sleeping with Serena would probably turn into the best mistake I had ever made.

Unfortunately, though, the climax-induced high wasn't everlasting. As it started wearing off, I couldn't help but think getting laid had never felt so crippling before. Not because Serena had claws and fangs down under. On the contrary. She was a fury in the sack... in all the best ways possible. It had, by far, been the best casual sex I'd had in a while, which may just have been the problem. Part of me screamed to hold on to Rayven, to not ask Serena for yet another repeat. The other, possibly slightly bigger part, made things extremely hard... *Hard*... to not ask for things to be made less hard on future occasions. My heart and my libido *so* weren't speaking the same language.

"You're not a crier, are you?" Serena frowned as she propped herself up on one arm, eyeing me, making me wonder if I shouldn't have just stuck to sleeping with people who didn't know me and wouldn't bother trying to read me, not caring to know anything more than the rock star front.

"What makes you think I may be?" I turned my head to look at her, getting more comfortable.

"You usually have quite a bit to say." She chuckled. "You being this quiet is unusual."

"Just getting ready to doze off," I lied, not even feeling the slightest bit bad about it.

"All right," she replied, shrugging it off as she snuggled into her pillow, clearly getting ready to call it a day herself. It was crazy how glad I felt about her not seeming to be much of a cuddler.

"That's a pretty wordless way of kicking somebody out." I laughed, not moving.

"Nah, you can stay. Just don't make fuckin' breakfast in the morning. No girlfriending moves."

"You got it. No girlfriending," I repeated amusedly, waiting until her breathing had evened out before I grabbed my phone off the floor to type out some lyrics.

Gotta grab inspiration by the balls when it hits you...

And, apparently, the muse responsible for an extra track for our album had just kissed me, or fucked me senseless.

Serenading Sins

She wears a golden cross around her neck,
But when she opens her mouth... Oh shit!
[Oh shit! Oh shit!]
She cusses like a sailor on a wreck – or crack.
I think she'll be my next hit.
[Hot damn, shit!]

But even a Serenade
Can feel like a hand grenade,
Hot like hell,
But is it all an empty shell?
[Hell no]
She's got a great personality,
But can't make dreams reality.

Friends with benefits,
Messing around like kids.
These words feel like bile
'Cause this really ain't my style.
It used to be,
But then you made me see
Sometimes being sappy
Is what can make you happy.
No one ever feels like you.
You keep me from startin' something new.
[Can't make dreams reality]

Even a Serenade
Can feel like a hand grenade.
She's a firecracker,
Yet the bang makes everything feel blacker.

I wish my heart had a switch.
Your memory is giving me a twitch.
You got under my skin.
Why does it feel like such a sin?
Trying to move on
From this phenomenon.

I have to move on, dear.
This is the last shed tear.

Even a Serenade
Can feel like a hand grenade.
She's my cuppa tea,
But you're my shot o' whiskey.
I'm drunk on you,
Giving me balls so blue.
[Can't sober up]
She's a firecracker,
Yet the bang makes everything feel blacker.

Chapter 13

"I *was thinking more along the* lines of something a little more... upbeat? More aggressive?" I offered with a look toward Chuck behind the drums. He was the best one to ask when it came to having someone guide us through the process of creating a song's rhythm.

It was a common misconception that bands like us just woke up with a perfect song in their heads every other morning. We took pride in writing and composing everything ourselves, and while some songs literally did come to us overnight, those were the exception. Much of our music was carefully crafted, absorbing a lot of creative energy, and we sometimes spent days at a time in the studio. No showers, no sunlight, lots of take-out food and crumpled up pieces of paper. We weren't going to deliver anything we hadn't poured our hearts into, no matter how much time it took. None of us cared about management chewing our asses enough to be willing to sacrifice our artistic integrity.

"Like this?" Chuck asked, putting his drumsticks into motion.

"Yeah, that's more the pace of it." I nodded. "The slower beat would have probably made y'all ask me how many cans of sob soup I've eaten again."

"Can we go through the vocals once more to get an idea of the actual melody?" Jake threw in, running his hand along the neck of his bass, smirking cheekily. "So we can un-sappy you."

"Yeah, let's go over it again," Jimmy agreed, picking up one of the copies we had made so each of us could have an eye on the lyrics. "How about you pick up an acoustic, Trent? When Owen did the first run-through to give us an idea, it kinda sounded like an extra guitar may work better than the keyboard."

"I was thinking the same thing." Trent nodded, grabbing his guitar from the corner of the small studio, making sure it was tuned right as he sat down, attaching a capo a moment later. It was great that all of us knew how to play the guitar to some extent. That way, we could rotate a little and make sure we got the best sound for any song we were working on.

"Ready to throw in some ideas?" Chuck smirked, counting up to four before setting the beat, the rest of the guys joining in soon after. Much like when we were teenagers and played in my parents' garage, I always looked forward to our jam sessions. Nothing beat creative collaboration.

Once I felt like they had come up with something solid and steady, I cleared my throat a bit and started singing as they adjusted their chords, strums, tabs, and beats. We kept repeating the process until we were all happy with the result, recording our progress to ensure we would be able to recreate our favorite results with ease.

You're the reason my heart skips a beat.
What I'd give for your skin against my sheet.
My feelings for you I can't deny.
[I won't fuckin' try!]
I wish your wings hadn't made you fly.
I thought I'd crushed your world, but you shattered mine.
Why can't we... Oh, why can't we go back in time?
Don't think that I wanna unmeet you,
But if that's all the time we got,
I wish we could just have another shot.

I wanna kiss you,
Not miss you.
Why does it have to feel this way
Every single day?
[Every fuckin' day]
Your wings... They made you fly.
Oh, tell me, does it sometimes make you cry?
[Baby, don't cry]

Does being apart put a tear in your eye?

Please tell me we didn't miss our last goodbye!

[Is this the last goodbye?]

Please come back.

Like an ant on crack,

You flew so high.

[So high]

Is this the last goodbye?

[The last goodbye]

Please come back.

Like an ant on crack,

Assemble the pieces, fix the heart.

It could be a brand new start.

[Or is this the last goodbye?]

"What's a flying ant on crack?" Jake asked after what should be our last run-through, at least for the time being, voicing the question I had expected to be asked after the first.

"Consider it artistic license... abstract art." I smiled in response, making Jimmy laugh.

"How come *he* gets to know and we don't?" Jake asked with a pout, picking up one of the paper balls and throwing it at Jimmy.

"No need to fight, kids. He just happens to remember more random shit than anyone else in this room." I shook my head. "Let's just say it all boils down to *her*."

"Which is why we're doing this whole thing in the first place." Trent nodded. "Didn't you say you had another song prepared for us, though?"

"Uh, yeah," I admitted quietly, running a hand through my already disheveled hair.

"Why suddenly so shy?" Chuck threw in. Most likely, he was just attempting to tease me, trying to get some sort of reaction, but all he got was a little glare.

"It's, uhm, kinda about someone you all know."

"No shit, Sherlock. Every fuckin' song that's going on this album is." Jimmy laughed, stopping just as abruptly as he had started, realization hitting him. "You're not referring to RayRay, are you?"

"Uh, no." I shook my head, getting out my phone and pulling up the lyrics I had written after the night with my favorite tattoo artist, handing it to Jimmy.

"Hey, why does he get to know?" Jake asked, repeating his earlier question.

"Knowing Jimmy, everyone else will in about three seconds. I'll be sending the lyrics to the printer in a minute, too. I just wanted to... give y'all a fair warning, I suppose," I offered awkwardly, still not entirely sure what to think of the whole thing myself.

Thing. Serena and I hadn't even established if it would be a repeating or a one-time thing, so how the hell was I supposed to bring up our non-thing thing with my friends?

"*O-m-g! Alert the media! Somebody finally got laid again!*" Jimmy yelled after reading the words on the screen. I was sure whoever was in the next studio must have heard him, as well. "Serena Maroney – turning blue balls golden!"

"I doubt that'll be her slogan anytime soon," I chuckled softly, rubbing my neck.

"So you and Serena, huh?" Trent asked, eyeing me a bit. "Can't say we didn't see that one coming."

"We're not in a relationship or anything. We're just two consenting adults doing... adult things."

"Rrrrrright," Jake laughed. "And you'll keep doing them, then you'll start staying at each other's places more frequently, then you'll start forgetting stuff at her place, and vice versa. It'll be put into drawers, and before you know it, you'll have a ring on it."

"You're one to talk," Trent scoffed. "You're the one who fucked us all for fake Elvis."

"Gangbang!" Jimmy exclaimed, making everyone in the room look at him like he was crazy. Smiling innocently, he shrugged and put down his guitar. "I don't like it when Mommy and Daddy fight."

"Soooo... Did you ask Serena if it was okay to mention her name?" Trent asked, grabbing the phone from Jimmy.

"I didn't... haven't. I mean, her name isn't even in it, so no." I shook my head, a bit surprised by the question. It wasn't like I was going to have her sign a fucking release for using a word that may have possibly once been a form of her name.

"*Serenade?* Don't you think that's close enough?" he chuckled, passing the phone to Chuck, which made me roll my eyes.

"He's right, dude." Chuck nodded in agreement. "It's only a two letter difference and obvious to anyone who knows her. You sure you wanna word it like that?"

"It's a nice way to say that words can hurt like a knife. Lyrics can be weapons, too, don't you think? 'Serenades feeling like hand grenades'? Plus, it truthfully plays on the inspiration for the song, so I don't see anything wrong with it."

"She'll cut off your dick and use it to hold a lampshade," Jake warned, making me chuckle involuntarily.

To be fair, his words made my cojones want to retreat far enough to hide behind my eyeballs, but I wouldn't have put it past her, and couldn't help imagining dick lamps decorating her shop.

"I wouldn't think it was funny if it were my junk we were talking about," Jake frowned, shaking his head.

"All right, well..." I sighed. "Basically, what you're saying is that if I were to sleep with a girl named Sushi – let her be a Susi with a lisp for all I care – I would never be allowed to say 'I'm gonna go eat Sushi' again without asking her permission first?"

"Depends on the context." Jimmy laughed, making Chuck choke on a sip of water.

"Seriously, though." I grabbed my phone so I could send the lyrics to the printer. "Almost all the songs on the album are related to Rayven in some way or another. The album itself is called *Rayvenous*, spelled just like her name. Did you see me go and ask her to give consent for us to use it? No? Well, Serena's name is being used just as fictitiously as Rayven's, and both of them have been abstracted well enough, if you ask me."

"That, kind sir, was quite the speech. Chapeau." Jimmy smirked, saluting me.

"Serena's a big girl. If she has a problem with the song, she'll deal with it," I mumbled, grabbing the printouts from the machine in the corner of the room.

"I'm not sure which I like better. This you, or the you desperately in need of a good fuck," Trent said. It sounded like he was joking, but I wasn't sure just how much honesty his words actually held. I knew I could be a little prissy when it came to all things Rayven, and as a distraction, Serena was, more or less, like a Rayven extension.

"So when are you going to see her again?" Trent asked. "Lyric said Serena'd stayed over last week or something?"

"*Lyric* said, huh?" I asked, eyeing him a bit. "Maybe we should refrain from mentioning any pillow talk in here before someone loses an eye."

"So you're the only one allowed to be hung up on someone?" Trent snorted.

The air felt charged, sizzling with energy, and I was almost certain punches would be thrown any moment. The rest of the band seemed to be convinced of the same, judging by the fact that Chuck and Jake started to get the instruments out of the way, lining them up by the walls.

Smart move.

"Hung up? *You're* the one who's been fucking my sister after years of promising you wouldn't touch her!"

"Maybe we should all go take a breather. Have a smoke. Say hello to daylight and goodbye to the lack of oxygen in here," Jake suggested, one hand already on the doorknob, ready to bolt if he had to. If I were him, I wouldn't have wanted to get caught in between Trenton and me, either.

"No. You know what?!" I asked, agitated. "I'll just call her and ask, so we can forget it ever was an issue."

"Lyric?"

I really hoped I only imagined Trent's face paling as he asked because having to get into a serious fight with him for mistreating my twin sister was the last thing I needed. Or wanted. If he had hurt my sister, though, there would be no way around turning his balls into a fucking mobile and hanging it from the ceiling.

"No...," I ground out. "Serena."

With an annoyed sigh, I searched for her name in my contacts, clicking it, making the mistake of turning on the speaker so everyone could hear.

"Sup? Are your pants calling mine?" Her voice dripped with amusement, making the guys laugh. She probably hadn't expected me to call, at least not so soon. Quite frankly, I hadn't planned to, either. Not yet. "Am I on speaker, douchebag? Dude, you're not running for president. I'm sure you don't have to trump one another with locker room talk."

"I'm not gonna ask you to brag about how amazing I am, though I'm sure you could," I chuckled, figuring humor was the best way out. "They want you to confirm that it's okay for me to put the word *serenade* in one of the new songs."

"Linked to sex," Chuck commented, making me roll my eyes for the umpteenth time that day.

It could have all gone so smoothly.

"Huh?" The confusion in Serena's voice would have been hard to miss. "What does that have to do with me?"

"Serena, serenade... They think it's about you," I said dryly. "So they want me to be a good boy and ask permission."

"That sounded so fuckin' dirty," Jimmy chuckled, probably enjoying the whole exchange more than anyone. Sometimes it seemed as if he were striving for other people's awkwardness, like it nurtured him. Not that I could blame him. I had been the same when it came to our interviewer for that talk show.

"Dude, that's how Lorelei got the sailors. How the Harpies lured in their boy toys. I'm all for it. Don't expect me to ask every time someone comes in to get something remotely music related tatted, though," she chuckled, "or chicken nuggets."

"You saw that, huh?"

"It's all over the internet. Can we please go to some kind of fast food restaurant and order six cunt nuggets with ketchup?"

"She's gross." Trent frowned before directing the same remark to my phone, as if he had just realized she could hear him. "You're gross."

"Tell me about it," Serena said dryly, hanging up on us without another word.

"Are we all happy now?" I asked dryly, shoving my phone back into my pocket.

"You weren't going to mention the dirty part of the lyrics, were you?" Trent asked, watching me with an unnerving expression I couldn't quite define.

"Shut up or I'll call my sister."

"To what? To tell her you don't approve of our relationship? That you don't want us dating, don't want me near her? Well, newsflash, Owen. We know. But we don't need your blessing."

Trent's calmness and how quiet the room had gotten were irritating me even more than it would have had he spit the words at me. I had never made my disapproval of their relationship a secret. Not because Trent was less of a brother to me than the rest of the guys, or because I thought Lyric or Trent – or Lyric *and* Trent – didn't deserve to be happy, but because I had watched both of them go through relationships, had seen them date, love, and suffer. I was there when Lyric got her heart broken for the first time, having to watch her reassemble the pieces. I witnessed Trenton change girlfriends like most people changed their underpants, hearing him, and – *shame on me* – sometimes even encouraging him to, brag about his conquests. I had watched them both make mistakes, had offered my sister a shoulder to cry on, and shared post break-up pints with my buddy.

In all honesty, though, it wasn't either one of them I was worried about. I knew they would be able to put the pieces back together if the other one crushed them. It was myself I was scared for. I didn't want to be the one in the middle, the one who would have to pick a side – which would, no doubt, be the ultimate consequence of their relationship derailing.

"Just... don't fuck up," I sighed quietly, running a hand through my hair. I hoped I wouldn't come to regret not blowing up at him, but I realized making them feel like they had to sneak around and hide wasn't fair.

"Whut?"

The surprise in Jake's voice made it sound as if he had the hiccups, incapable of using the correct vowel. Four sets of curious eyes stared back at me. I felt like there wasn't a right thing for me to say. Maybe they had been mentally preparing to give me a tongue-lashing for shutting Trent down, which I had failed to do, seemingly flabbergasting them.

"You heard me. It's not like I didn't know. But I don't want to end up having to serve Lyric his balls on a silver platter because he couldn't keep it zipped on the road."

"Dude, I'm not going to–" Trenton started, but I held up my hand, really not wanting to hear it.

"I know you're not going to deliberately hurt her, Trent, but that doesn't mean it won't happen. And if – or when – it does, I'm not gonna have much of a choice when it comes to picking sides."

"I get that." He nodded slowly, eyeing me. For a moment, I wasn't sure we wouldn't end up shoving our fists into each other's faces after all. "But you, of all people, also have to understand that nothing you could possibly say right now will change the way I feel about her."

"That's... surprisingly good to hear," I admitted, the corners of my lips tugging up.

"Now that we got that settled... Chop-chop." Jimmy smiled, clapping his hands. "Time to get back to work. We got an album to finish before the tour kicks off."

Chapter 14

"**O**h, *my god, oh, my* god, oh, my god, oh, my god! You said yes!" Lyric yelled, running down the stairs as soon as I had entered the house, all but flying toward me, wrapping her arms around my neck, as if we had something to celebrate. And I guess she kind of did.

"I, uhm... No need to go dress shopping," I offered jokingly, a little overwhelmed by her demeanor as I returned the hug, mostly to make sure she didn't fall onto her head. As her brother, I considered it my duty to say she didn't have any brain cells to spare.

"Yet," she smirked, squeezing me even tighter.

"Wait... What? You're not... *You* aren't the one who actually said yes to something, are you?"

"No, silly," Lyric laughed. I was surprised at how relieved that simple two-letter word made me feel. "But *you* didn't say no!"

"Are you referring to what I think you're referring to?" I asked slowly, thinking it was best to make sure we were on the same page, that we weren't getting our wires crossed. Considering the very un-librarian life I had lived – no offense to any book treasurers out there – things could have become awkward rapidly had one of us been talking about ice cream and the other about colonoscopies... just to name a rather implausible blend of subject matters.

"Trent and I are now *officially* a thing." She beamed, letting go of me and getting back onto her own two feet. "Thank you, thank you, thank you."

"I, uh... I'm not part of that relationship," I replied reluctantly, clearing my throat, "and I didn't exactly say yes. I just told him not to fuck up."

"That's kind of the same difference, Ow. He pretty much called me the moment you left the studio, even more excited than I am about not having to tiptoe around as much anymore. I can actually go on tour with you guys now, and–"

"L, *no*. No tour bus shenanigans. Just... No."

"Gee, bro. Relax." She shook her head, actually having the nerve to laugh. "I wasn't saying we would do the road humpehdy-dumpehdies. And stop calling me 'L'. It makes me sound like an eighty-year-old."

Lyric was probably the only person who could, just by being herself, make me feel like the sanest person in the world – which said a lot, considering I had believed Rayven's stories rather than choosing to think rationally and being convinced she had just hit her head. And I still kind of did believe her, so maybe I was the one who'd been hit on the head. Hard. By a jumbo jet.

Just as I was about to reply to her rather crude remark about making the bus bounce, our mother's voice rang from behind me, saying something I had *never* wanted to hear coming from her.

"Wouldn't be the first time," she said amusedly, playfully slapping me on the back of the head as she passed. There they went, my precious brain cells, which explained so many things. "Can't blame your sister for anything you'd do. Worse yet, anything you *have* done."

"Stop speaking words of wisdom, Mom." I chuckled softly. "Gotta take care of my little sister, don't I?"

"She's less than ten minutes younger than you, Owen, and I'm pretty sure that's only because the doctor just grabbed you first, instead of attaching that plumber-like tool to *her* head."

"Ouch." I frowned, although I had insanely missed our family dynamics. My mother had gotten pregnant young, so it was sometimes as if she barely had any years on us – especially mentally. Jokingly, as Lyric walked by, I muttered, "Best seven minutes of my life."

"I'm her favorite," she smiled sweetly, following our Mom into the kitchen, "which is also why I have the prettier name, even though guys can be named Lyric, too."

"Such a waste," I sighed dramatically, grabbing a cookie as soon as Mom set them down on the counter. "*Dumbfuck* would've done just as nicely."

"Owen Connors, watch your mouth, or you'll be chewing on a bar of soap."

"Mom, please," Lyric laughed. "His band's called The Cunt-Nuggets, and every other word he forces on those poor people involuntarily listening to one of their songs on the radio is 'fuck'."

"Speaking of fucking and being forced to hear things...," I grumbled, hoping my dismay was as present in my voice as it was in the pit of my stomach. "What was that supposed to mean, exactly? 'Wouldn't be the first time'?"

"I am sure that bus of yours has seen more naked bodies than it would care to admit... had it the ability to speak." Mom smiled softly, way too calm, considering the topic we were discussing. "You, the other guys, the girls you've brought along, the girls the other guys invited in, *Lyric*..."

"*Mom!*" Lyric gasped. "You weren't supposed to tell!"

"This just got mighty interesting," I said matter-of-factly, grabbing as many cookies as I could hold before letting myself fall into one of the kitchen chairs. "Please, go on, continue."

"I'd prefer Trent's parts to keep functioning, thank you very much." Lyric frowned, still glaring at our mother, who seemed to find the situation way too amusing. We definitely found ourselves in one of those very rare moments where I would have preferred to have a much more conservative parental figure. And, judging by her behavior, Lyric would have one hundred percent agreed with me. Then again, she didn't have to tell our mother, of all people, about her sexual adventures.

"Oh, no fuckin' way. I ain't touching his junk," I replied around a mouthful of cookie crumbs. Ironically, that was what my mother glared at me for. So her daughter sleeping with a dude who made music for a living wasn't an issue, yet me talking with my mouth full obviously was?

"Not like you'd have to touch it."

"True. I could just, you know, send him to a vet, have them castrate him like a guinea pig. I once saw this thing on TV. They just put the little piggy on its back, gave it a local anesthesia, poked the balls with a scalpel once they'd found them, and then just squee-"

"*Owen!*" Mother all but growled. "You shut your cakehole. Your sister is just as much entitled to a love life as you are. At least she picked someone I know and am comfortable with."

"You're... *comfortable* with Trenton?" I cleared my throat, trying really hard not to double over laughing. "Is that the same Trent I know?"

"You're just jealous because you scare your nights' leftovers away before you can have seconds," Lyric smirked. That time, she was the one our mother tossed a kitchen towel at, shushing her.

"I'll be in the basement, doing laundry, before one of you gives me a heart attack. Cardiac arrest isn't exactly on my to-do list today. Ain't nobody got time for that." She shook her head as she walked past my sister and me, smiling. "You kids behave. My house, my rules."

"I don't think Serena would mind seconds. Actually, we had more than seconds the other night," I countered dryly once Mom had left the room. I didn't need her getting excited over having Serena around more often, when the "more often" would have been limited to overnight shagging sessions or daylight dirties.

"Wait... What?" I wasn't sure she had even tried to, but Lyric didn't do a very good job of hiding her surprise. At all. "I thought nothing happened!"

"Not *that* night, no." I shrugged casually. "Doesn't mean it hasn't since."

"So, are you and her...?"

"Fucking? Yeah."

"Owen!"

What was it with the ladies in my life constantly scolding me for saying one thing or another? Hadn't she, just moments before, reminded the boss of the house of the vocabulary used in most of our songs? Had defended my wording based on my profession? And now she, herself, sounded like our mother.

"Hasn't anyone taught you how to treat a lady?"

"Serena is no lady," I scoffed. "If she caught you calling her one, she would probably promise to outlive you just so she could piss on your grave."

"I like her," Lyric protested, crossing her arms like a little kid who'd just been denied a trip to the zoo. The only thing missing was her stomping a foot to emphasize her point.

"I do, too..." I made it sound more like a question than an actual reply.

"But you just said you were fucking. Don't you think that's a little...

I don't know... crude? Kind of makes her sound like a worthless whore."

"Nope. We agreed we weren't *girlfriending*. At all. No relationship, no strings. We're not in love, so don't even go anywhere near thinking it should be called 'making love'. What do you want me to call it?"

"Me? I'm not the one you're–"

"Fucking." I smirked, moving my eyebrows up and down, slowly eyeing her.

"Gross!"

"Yeah, I don't like what I'm seeing, either." I chuckled, my words making her groan. "Seriously, though, L. Don't hype it. We're just... blowing off steam."

"Don't even start to say that one of you is taking the blowing more literal than the other. I don't wanna know."

"I like the way your mind works, little Connors. You have been taught well."

"It's not nearly as corrupted as yours," Lyric said, sounding a little snotty. She grabbed a freezer bag from one of the drawers and started filling it with cookies.

"You're dating one of my best friends, who can be a total pig, so there's no way in heaven, hell, or on Earth your mind's any less fucked up than mine." I narrowed my eyes at her. "And don't fuckin' bring him my cookies!"

"They're not *yours*. Mom made them for all of us."

"Which means me, me, me, *you*, me, me, *herself*, and me. You can have all the cookies in the world when I'm not home. Now that

I have to share my friend with you, you can't expect me to share my *cookies* with him."

"Dude, you sound like one of the *Gilmore Girls*. Sharing is caring. You should have learned that in the womb."

"Right." I watched her put the bag full of baked goodness into her purse. "*You're* probably the one to blame for the way I am. I mean, look at you. Taking my friend. Taking my cookies. You probably used to suck up all the nourishment that was supposed to come down my umbilical cord before it could ever reach me. You made me a green-eyed monster before I ever saw the cold light of day."

"Wow, dramatic much, aren't we?"

"What can I say? I'm an artist, a musician. A fragile little soul."

"What you are is so full of shit, I'm afraid you're gonna burst and make the mess of the century." She chuckled, swinging her bag over her shoulder as she paraded toward the door to the garage. "Don't wait up, sucker. I'm about to screw the brains out of your buddy."

I groaned as she shut the door. She was going to pay for that one.

Chapter 15

"**D**ude... *Here,*" *I said without* any preceding greeting a few days later, shoving a small folder at Trent as he was about to leave our place. He had spent time with Lyric – in her room, with the door closed – so I made sure to remain downstairs as much as possible, not wanting to see or hear anything that would have made me even more prone to shake him down for some of his most treasured body parts. I narrowed my eyes at him. "Is that my shirt?"

"What's this?" Trent sounded genuinely curious, his eyebrows moving up enough to almost fade into his hairline as he opened the folder, his eyes wandering down the first page.

"I asked if that was my shirt." Smirking, I watched him, chuckling when he called me a smartass. We were used to sharing on the road – it broadened your wardrobe when you weren't limited to wearing your own clothes. To be fair, inquiring about his outfit hadn't been the purpose of intercepting his attempted escape.

"'Rules for Dating My Sister'? Really?" he scoffed, falling onto the sofa next to me, skimming through the pages before going back to the first one. *"'You break her heart, I'll break your everything, except your instruments. They're good. We'll keep them. Might make it easier to replace your sorry ass. Right now, I am saying that lovingly – in a non-gay way. Break her heart, and it's enunciated with your every enemy's vengeful bitterness, though.'"* He looked up at me. "Seriously, man?"

"C'mon, keep reading." I nodded at the paper, trying not to laugh. His facial expression was a heavenly combination of irritated, amused, and incredulous. Shaking his head, he stared at me for a moment before letting out a defeated sigh.

"'Don't make her cry. If I see her shed so much as one single unhappy tear because of you, I'll make sure every future meal of yours is seasoned with crushed salt and vinegar chips. I know how much you hate that shit. Beverages, too. Mmmm, yummy! Salt and Vinegar Chip Crumble Hot Chocolate. If it becomes a hipster thing, though, I'm going all "all rights reserved". My idea. Can't take credit for it.'"

If he had looked incredulous while reading the first point eternalized in the document, he looked entirely alienated after having read the second part. "What the ever-loving fuck is this shit, man?"

"A guidebook." I tried to sound proud, despite the chuckle I just hadn't been able to hold in. "There are five more pages, as I am sure you've noticed."

"Salt and Vinegar Chip Crumble? What kind of fucked-up barista have you been bagging?"

"At that point in time, I wasn't *bagging* anyone," I snickered, nodding toward the folder. "My barely even fifteen-year-old self put that together."

His eyes widened. "So you've had this shit for more than half a decade?" Trent frowned, looking back down at the folder. "Back then, Lyric and I weren't even close to..."

"Banging?" I deadpanned, really wishing he had simply finished his sentence with "dating", or anything, rather than giving me the opportunity to do it for him.

"You know what I mean."

"If I could be sure of it, I wouldn't have had to carefully compose what you've been referring to as 'this shit'." Smirking, I shook my head. "Besides, it doesn't have your name on it. Don't flatter yourself. Could've been written for anyone."

"It mentions salt and vinegar chips, Owen. How many fuckin' people have told you they are grossed out by their mere existence? They're not like... peas. Or cabbage. Or spinach. Or even fuckin' asparagus. They're nothing people would randomly list as their least favorite food item."

"Touché, but that's as obvious as you and Lyric have always been."

"But back then we weren't... I mean..."

"You were majorly bummed when Lyric announced she wanted to spend a year abroad. She started applying when we were fifteen. You majorly crushing on her was just as obvious back then as it has been the past few years."

"But you never said anything."

"What did you expect me to say? 'Oh, hey, you fancying my sister?'"

"I don't know. Something. Anything. Would've been nice to know how you'd felt about it, I guess."

"Is it? Nice to know, I mean?"

"I suppose not. Not really." Trent chuckled nervously, running a hand through his hair. "Gotta do double duty to watch out for her, since your dad's not around much, huh?"

"This has nothing to do with having an absentee parent and everything to do with her being my sister and you being one of my best friends. If one of you fucks up, what the hell am I supposed to do? Tell her everything will be all right, while at the same time telling you you'll find someone better? You'd both expect me to take sides, and I'm pretty sure neither taking sides nor pretending to be Switzerland would be as easy as it sounds."

"Right." He grimaced, giving me the impression that, despite having tried to hide it from me for so long, he hadn't really considered, or come to understand, what consequences their relationship, and especially a potential failure thereof, could really have on me, someone who would end up being the piggy in the middle, so to speak.

"I know I've been selfish, letting you both know time and time again how little I wanted you two to be together. And believe me, the egoistic bastard in me still doesn't want to *ever* get close to being in a situation where he'll have to pick between his sister and one of his brothers."

"Is there going to be a but?" Trent asked, his voice, as well as the way he looked at me, reminding me of the hopefulness you saw in shelter dogs that had been waiting to be adopted for far too many days. I couldn't help wondering if I hadn't been a tad too cruel regarding Lyric and him, but...

"Yeah..." I shrugged, nodding a bit and taking a deep breath. "*But* I've also had to go through the whole wanting someone you can't have thing. I've kinda gotten stuck there. Owen Connors, forever in relationship purgatory. I don't want either one of you to break the other's heart... but I also don't wanna be the one doing it for you. So, be my guest. Do whatever you want, not like you haven't been doing just that anyway. But keep the salt and vinegar chips in mind. Forever. And. Always."

"I love those." Lyric smiled, rounding the corner and all but jumping into Trent's lap. I should have known better than to assume she had been upstairs in her room and out of earshot.

"Those things are gross." Trent frowned as I watched his hand land on her thigh, his arm around her. I narrowed my eyes at him, probably looking like a hawk stalking its next prey.

"Are not. The friend who kept calling you cunt nuggets? She introduced me to them when I was in Europe. I'd never wanted to try them before, either, but they are so... fucking... good."

"You two are what's gross." With an overly dramatic sigh, I got up, wrinkling my nose at Trent. "I thought you were leaving."

"That was before your sister decided to abuse our newly acquired right of public display of affection in this house," he smirked, burying his nose in her hair.

"Again, gross. I'm sure she hasn't washed that mane in at least three months."

"I have been eyewitness and accomplice in getting her as clean as can be on more than one occasion in said timeframe."

Watching Lyric laugh at him, playfully slapping his arm, made it hard to keep my lips from starting to tug up into a smile I didn't want either one of them to see. If each other was what they really needed, wanted, then who was I to be a jerkish obstacle?

"And that's Owen over and out, ladies and gentlemen."

"Outchie! Where are you going?" Lyric called after me as I made my way toward the door, grabbing my keys from the little cabinet in the hallway. God, I hated that nickname. It was even worse than Owey. But, hey, since she'd felt the need to ask...

"I'm gonna pick up Serena to go down 69 V-Line Trail," I replied, trying to keep the smirk out of my voice. I had already started a mental countdown, waiting for my sister to make a remark regarding my response.

3... 2... aaaand...

I chuckled when realization must have hit her, a loud "Ewwww!" echoing from the room I had just left.

Trent's laughter at her reaction made the corners of my lips tug up even more. At least he hadn't started censoring his dirty mind around her. It would have been a shame for him to lose his somewhat twisted sense of humor that made him fit right in with the rest of us.

"And he says *we're* the gross ones," she complained, the disgust evident in her voice as I closed the door behind me.

Chapter 16

"**S**erena, what's up?" *I called* as I entered her tattoo shop a little while later, possibly... no, *positively* with the previously declared intention. After all, the best way to stop the mind's wheels from churning was to let the blood flow to different, less intellectually productive body parts, and having seen Lyric and Trent all lovey-dovey definitely called for a distraction. Not just because they were my sister and one of my best friends, but also – and especially – because it was, kinda-sorta, pretty much what I so desperately wanted, but couldn't have. I wanted the girl I had fallen in love with to just fall from the sky so we could be what Trenton and Lyric were: Together in the most sickeningly, cheesy way humanly possible.

"Hopefully not you because some of us gotta work for a living," she replied, her voice dripping with amusement, the familiar, calming buzz of her tattoo machine filling the air.

"You *so* didn't just say that!" a second female exclaimed with a giggle, prompting Serena to sigh in exasperation, lifting the needle away from the girl's skin just as I rounded the corner, stepping behind the screen shielding one of the workstations from curious glances.

"How about some privacy?" Serena huffed, rolling her eyes back so far, she was probably able to check out her own ass – which would have been a view to be jealous of.

"Do you mind...?" I looked at the girl sitting there.

"Bethany," she breathed, a slight pink blush spreading over her cheeks. Either she knew who I was or she was just smitten by my spectacular entrance... all hot and handsome. If you asked me, that description couldn't be called a made-up, exaggerated self-assessment. It was simply made up of feedback I had gotten repeatedly. I certainly hoped I hadn't gotten arrogant enough to label *myself* a hotshot.

"Well, Bethany, do you mind?" I repeated with the sweetest smile I could muster, which turned into a satisfied smirk as soon as she started to shake her head. "Great."

"Oh, please, like she had a choice. All you gotta do to drop some panties is to pop those dimples," Serena sighed, starting to work her artistic magic on her client's skin once again.

It wasn't like Bethany was getting her hooha or her nips inked. It was a shoulder blade tattoo, she was still wearing a bra, *and* her front was against the chair she sat on so Serena would have better access to the girl's back. I really wasn't sure exactly what Serena thought I could be getting a kick out of.

"Wait... So you two are...? You know...?" Bethany asked, her teeth sinking into her bottom lip.

Her apparent insecurity, as well as the resulting reluctance, were cute. I couldn't help wondering if she and Serena would be opposed to sharing for, let's say, one instance of benefits. I was convinced I could have easily ensured neither one of them would have only gotten half the fun while I was getting double. In *that* regard, I may have actually been more convinced of myself than in the looks department previously mentioned. A lot. In my book, skill trumped looks any day.

I smirked. "Human? Yes. Of the same gender? No. Drunk? Not right now, although I can only speak for myself. Coffeeholics? I'd say we both consume our share. Burnt Ashes groupies? Again, I can only speak for myself, but I'd say Serena's probably drooled over one picture or another on more than one occasion..."

"Oh god. Trey Baker is so hot," Bethany gushed, making me raise an eyebrow. "I mean, he's nothing compared to you, *of course*, but... Yum."

"He is," Serena agreed, "and he has a very moanable name."

"Hey now," I pouted. "Last time I checked, you didn't have any problems with the 'Ohhhh' in the beginning of *my* name, either. Don't get your bands mixed up."

"So you two *are*...?" Bethany tried again, daring to peek at Serena over her shoulder, despite being in the process of getting permanently marked, which usually had people sitting still rather than twisting and turning.

"We're not dating, no." Serena spoke before I had the chance to reply, though the rest of her response truly surprised me. "Fucking, though? Hell yeah."

Clearly at a loss for words, Bethany murmured something indistinguishable, causing Serena and me to trade an amused glance.

———◆———

"You can't just barge in here like that," Serena sighed as she wiped down her space, freeing her utensils from any germs that could possibly contaminate her working environment.

"Why not?"

Smirking, I watched her throw away used paper towels, preparing everything for her next client, who, unfortunately, wasn't going to be me. New ink wasn't the distraction I'd come for, but adding to the masterpiece my skin had started to become was never *not* an option. Ever. But would I really choose coming for a tattoo over coming from something else... coming *for* someone else, so to speak... if presented the option? Depending on my current mood and mindset, maybe. That very moment? Doubtful, although Serena had said I'd better not be the one up...

"Because I have a job. This is where I work. And it's not the place to look for a lap lassie."

"Chill your nips, cupcake. All I did was stop by. For all you know, I could have come by for a consultation or to look through your wanna-dos – even if your wants didn't include me – to see if anything made my skin tingle. *You* were the one who made an insinuating comment."

"Remotely," she retorted, prompting me to raise my eyebrows in disbelief. Had she not made a pantsy comment when I'd asked her what was up?

"You were also the one who told Bethany all you needed were my dimples to pop for your panties to get drenched. Don't tell me that wasn't a salacious remark."

"I was joking," she replied, her words seeming almost sheepish, especially compared to her usual demeanor. "Didn't mean she needed confirmation about... this thing we have."

"I just went with it 'cause *you* seemed to." I sighed, running a hand through my hair. "If you're waiting for an apology, sorry, I guess, but–"

"Sorry, you guess? *If* I'm waiting for an apology?" she repeated, sounding like she was anything but content with my wording. Couldn't blame her, I suppose, but what had she expected? For me to apologize for the way a conversation had gone, which she'd been just as much a part of as I had, with an equal amount of opportunity to influence it? To change its course?

"Weren't *you* the one to confirm the actual fuckery happening? You could have labeled my part of the conversation just as much a joke as yours... until you said we were fucking, without leaving any room for interpretation."

"Whatever, Connors. This is dumb."

Taking a deep breath, I rubbed my neck, watching her intently. She couldn't be serious. How had we gone from a no strings attached, benefits-included friendship to it actually being a "thing we're having", then calling the "thing we're having" dumb?

"I thought this was a no drama thing," I carefully tried after a moment of silence. "What's going on here, Serena?"

"Nothing," she sighed, fidgeting with one of those little rubber pots used to hold ink. "Sorry. I guess I'm just... I have a lot going on right now."

"Is that a way to say we should call things off?"

It surprised me how posing that question made me feel. It wasn't exactly panic, but it most certainly also wasn't indifference. I felt reluctance, and I wasn't sure how to feel about that, either. I wasn't in love with Serena, but I dreaded the possibility of losing the way things were. Comfortable, yet exciting. No drama whatsoever, prior to that day, yet not calm enough to be boring. And, to be fair, distraction enough to give me breaks from beating myself up over Rayven, breaks from mourning her disappearance without forcing me to let go.

"You can't call something off that isn't really a thing, can you?" she asked. I would be lying if I said her evading my question didn't make my heart skip a beat.

"I suppose not." I nodded slowly, unable to really form a coherent thought. Did that mean she was or wasn't putting an end to our non-thing thing?

"There you go then," Serena scoffed, making a move to walk past me, but I gently grabbed her wrist to stop her.

"Is that what this is about then? You wanting it to be an actual...
thing?" I probed, unsure whether or not I even wanted her to answer
that question. For fuck's sake, I wasn't even sure how I would have
answered it myself.

"Do you?"

Of course she had to ask, biting her lip and looking up at me
through her eyelashes, giving me one of those not-even-that-cute
dollish looks girls liked to use when they didn't want to be told no.
Great. So that had been a "yes" on her part, which still didn't mean I
had an appropriate answer.

"I..."

"You don't... wouldn't, would you?"

"Serena, I like you. A lot. I like spending time with you, and I like
what we've got going on here... whatever it is. But I don't think I can
give you what you want. This has been... *is* great, but I'm not sure it's
a good idea to label this because-"

"I'm not her," she whispered, using words I never would have. At
least not out loud. But had my mental wording actually been all that
different from her spoken one? Not really. Yet I didn't feel like agreeing
with her because that would have meant hurting her, something I had
no intention of doing, even if we'd probably set ourselves up to do
exactly that. Not agreeing or disagreeing, though, would have come as
close to a lie as possible, which would have hurt her sooner or later, too.

"You're taking way too long to think your answer over," Serena sighed. "I know we've been playing with open cards all along, but..."

"But you're not as tough as you always seem?" I offered softly, brushing back a strand of her hair with the hand that wasn't holding hers to keep her from walking away. Not that she would've wandered farther than one room.

"Neither are you," she replied with a slight chuckle. "What are we doing, Owen?"

"I honestly don't know anymore. Whatever it is, I like it... but part of me still hopes to find her again. As amazingly awesome as you are, Serena, I think I'll be forever stuck on 'there's no replacing her'. I'm like a broken record. My head says I need to finally find a way to move on, instead of just seeking distraction, but my heart keeps telling my head to fuck off." I smirked, trying to lighten the mood a bit again. "And my dick's a whole other story."

Cocking an eyebrow, she playfully slapped my chest. "That one's the one that likes me, huh?"

"You have no idea how much." I nodded, tongue in cheek. "But the rest of me does, too. Every fiber in my body says 'no' to even attempting anything labeled as a relationship, though. That's nothing I can apologize for, if you want me to mean it."

"So you like the way things are?"

"I'm well aware you and I go together like whiskey and ginger ale, Serena. This *friendship* has the most excellent benefits. It's just not the same."

"Big 'ewww' to that combination of drinks. You could have done way better there. What if you never find her again, though? Are you planning to be a crazy old cat dude then? Creepy Uncle Owen?"

"I'm more of a dog person," I laughed, glad things had quickly gotten a little more color again. "But yeah. No. Maybe. I'm working on it, believe me. This whole new album was supposed to be my way of getting it all out, writing it off my soul and giving myself a chance to start over... after one last try."

"I can wait one last try, if that's what it takes."

She nodded, making my insides churn a bit. It was great that she wanted to give us an actual chance once I was, if ever, ready for it, but the fact she'd basically made it sound like there was no way in hell for me to find Rayven again didn't sit so well with me. In my book, chances being slim didn't make them non-existent. I definitely wasn't ready to give up yet, even after everything.

Guess I'm a hopeless case.

"We're okay then? Without any changes?"

"I... Yeah. Under one condition," Serena agreed reluctantly, pulling away so she could leave the room to get her sketchpad. "There's a certain something going on that I'll need to show stability for. Stability in my life. So, if you come waltzing in here at the wrong time, don't make a scene if I actually *do* refer to you as my 'boyfriend', even if you do, in reality, refuse to be labeled that way. Just... Play along then, 'kay?"

"I can do that... if you're sure someone like me actually adds to seeming stable." Her words piqued my curiosity. "What's the certain something?"

"*Something*," she emphasized, shaking her head, "I don't want to talk about. You don't want to talk about her. I don't want to talk about this. We both have a past we want to turn into our future, but before that actually happens, I guess they'll both stay locked up in their respective boxes."

"Let me know if that ever changes on your part. Good thing about people who don't want to talk about their own issues is that we're usually pretty good listeners."

"Likewise, Connors, likewise. Unless it's another drunken sob story about ants," she chuckled.

I could feel a frown tugging down the corners of my lips. I hadn't been aware I had shared *that* much of Rayven's short story that night up on Meadow Heights. Then again, I'd been more than just a little drunk by the end of the night, so who knows how much I'd actually ended up telling Serena.

"Don't worry. That's all part of what's inside *my* box. Locked up and covered in dust until its bearer of keys shows up... if she ever does."

Chapter 17

"Serena's such a girl," I sighed as I plopped down on Lyric's bed, forcing her to scoot over so her mattress could comfortably accommodate both of us.

"You know, Ow, knocking's not a voluntary option. I could have been naked."

"If I would have seen something I hadn't seen before, I promise I would have thrown a dollar or two at it."

Not that I would have been particularly fond of seeing my sister naked, but it could have been worse. She could have had a visitor, and both of them could have been naked. Again, none of it would have been news to my eyes separately, but the picture of the two of them together would have probably been forever burned into my memory...

as would the mental image the mere thought gave me.

"Charming," she replied dryly, "but I'm sure making it rain with two dollar bills would have been a unique view."

"Nothing but special for you, L. That's why you ended up with Trent, too. Because he's 'special'."

"Shut your muffin gap, Owen. What do you want?"

"Whine," I chuckled, getting more comfortable, which prompted her to kick me very un-accidentally.

"Go ahead and whine then, but take your filthy feet off my bed. They're probably covered in fungi and dick cheese."

"How the fuck would my feet be...? Never mind. I don't even want to know." Taking a deep breath, I rubbed my face. "Right now, I'm not sure whether I want to whine about Serena being such a girl, or if I should whine about you being you instead."

"Such a girl, hum? I wasn't aware you didn't know the gender of whom – or, rather, what – you were screwing. Usually you can tell by counting holes, if nothing else. Or by checking for a half-hidden elephant, peeking out from its hiding spot, its trunk hanging out..."

"You're such a fuckin' smartass." I chuckled. It must have been a dominant genetic trait. I had yet to meet a family member who wasn't entirely inclined to smartassery. She was. I was. Our mother was. And I'm pretty sure our grandmother was, even though she usually tried to hide it – probably because she didn't want to be a bad influence on us, not knowing all hope for that had been lost long ago.

"Oh, and, Ow? Speaking of fucking... These sheets haven't seen the washer since Trent last stopped by, so... you're welcome."

"I'm *welcome*? For what?" I frowned, not moving in the slightest. If she thought used sheets would make me jump to my feet, she was wrong – *so* wrong. "You didn't have to explain the anatomical features of females to me, though. I honestly doubt I need any help with that."

"Well... You did hint on her being a *girl* just now, making it sound like you hadn't known before, so unless you tell me what exactly you *do* need help with, I'll just keep saying things you don't want to hear. Like how to physically tell genders apart. Or how Trent and I mixed our juices all over these sheets."

"Lyric! Don't call it that. Seriously. Gross."

"Oh, I'm sorry if I'm the one making you all squeamish for a change. Roll reversal can be such a beautiful thing, don't you think?"

"You're seriously twisted, L."

"And you love it."

She had no idea how much. All the regular complaints aside, I really could have done worse for a sister. She could have turned into some Barbie doll dingy, with zero sense of humor, wrinkling her nose at anything not pink plush.

"So what's the current issue, oh beloved brother of mine?"

"Thanks for the sarcasm," I sighed, figuring I should share, though. After all, it had been the point in me coming in here, even if her words almost made me want to take back my former thought of how much I appreciated whoever's choice of making her my sister. *Almost.* "I think... No, I know... I think... I mean, I think I know–"

"Cut to the chase, will you?" Lyric chuckled. "I'm pretty sure what comes after all those verbs actually is the important part. I like a good story... once I've gotten past the monologue-ish prologue."

"Right, uhm... It seems Serena wants to put a label on us."

"Awwey, wittwle Owey's gwetting a gwirlfwiend," she responded, making me roll my eyes at the baby voice she used.

Oh Lord, have mercy... even if I'm far from religious.

"I don't think he is."

"Really?" she asked, almost sounding shocked, which surprised me. It wasn't like I had ever been the serious relationship type... except for once. "So you're cutting her loose? I thought you liked what you had."

"I did. I do."

"Then why?"

"You know why."

As if on cue, she let go of a sigh, shaking her head slightly, sounding disappointed in me.

Dramatic much. Thanks for teaching her that, Mom.

"Put her in the fine print then."

"This isn't some kinda contract, Lyric. How would you have reacted if Trent had handed you the terms and conditions of your relationship?"

"Aren't relationships, though? Contractual? You agree on terms, act accordingly... like no cheating, for example. So Trent and I actually *do* kinda have terms and conditions. Plus, if I remember correctly, *you* pretty much handed him an extension to those in written form."

"You're honestly saying I should... enter a relationship with fine print? Sounds like an emotional massacre waiting to happen. And how exactly would that be any different from how things are now? She's already in the fine print of... things, if you wanna put it like that."

"Right now, she's in a very bold, all caps fine print, though. And it'd make you two official, you and Serena. At least for now."

"But that also means there'd eventually be a breakup."

"Or not."

"Lyric..."

"You know, considering the amount of tattoos you have, one wouldn't think you had commitment issues."

"That's different. They don't talk. They don't want things certain ways. They're just there and look pretty. That's it."

"But they're permanent, like a girlfriend."

"Like a very quiet, pretty, always on my side of things girlfriend."

"Maybe you should date a blow-up doll then," Lyric deadpanned, her voice drier than the desert.

"I'm not into balloon animals painted like drag queens, thank you very much."

"I really don't know what you want, Owen. You want her, but you don't. You want to wait around for Rayven to make a miraculous reappearance, but you don't want to blue ball yourself. You want a relationship, but you don't want any strings. You want an easy breakup, but you want to be with an actual human being. You gotta get your wires uncrossed, dude."

"Right from the beginning, Serena and I *agreed* that was gonna be us, though, Lyric! We agreed there'd be no strings. We would just have fun and that'd be it. I told her, very clearly, that I wasn't looking for a fuckin' girlfriend!"

"Things change, Owen. Feelings evolve, people grow closer or apart. Maybe she has reached a point in her life where 'no strings' just doesn't work for her anymore. She's only human, too, you know."

"I hate when you make sense and I can't decide if I want to hug you or slap you."

"You can't slap me, Ow. I'm pretty close with your mother, and I'm sure she's taught you not to hit girls, especially when they're right." Lyric smiled. I couldn't help but laugh a little, despite how heated our conversation had started to get.

"Pretty close with my mother, huh?" I smirked, smacking her with a pillow.

"Uh-huh... I saw her from the inside once. Now, get the fuck out of here and don't come back until you know what you want."

"You're a creep, and a gross one, too." I chuckled. "And I'm not sure that'll ever happen."

"It better. I'm sure even Serena won't wait around forever."

"But... I'm fun between the sheets." I tried to sound a little pouty, but it was hard to stay serious when Lyric started using her feet to push me out of the bed.

"I don't want to fucking know. Gross. Get out!"

"You're the one who mentioned making 'fruit punch' with one of my friends, and *I'm* gross?" I laughed, half of my body already hanging over the edge of her bed, nearly falling out.

"Yes, because you just said you're fun between the sheets while in *my* bed! Now move it before I make you."

"You already started making me."

"Dude, that sounds so wrong," Lyric replied, cracking up. "Seriously, though, move it before we wake up Mom when your fat ass hits the floor!"

"Stop pushing me out then," I chuckled, grasping her blanket, as if that were by some miracle going to keep me from tumbling out of bed like a drunk toddler.

"We're not having a sleepover. Occasionally, I like having the bed all to myself."

"I'll go tell Trent." Smirking, I got up, throwing the blanket at her, covering her face.

"He knows. That's why he isn't here tonight," I heard her mumble as I walked out, the frown I had been sporting when walking into her room having turned into a smile, despite still facing the same issues. It sometimes wasn't so bad not being an only child.

Chapter 18

"*I swear to God, Ebby, he* all but ate me when I mentioned it. And I don't even mean that in a pleasurable way. More like a grizzly bear, all rawr-rawr-ing."

Being greeted by those words coming out of the next room was not what I had expected when I walked into Serena's place a few days later to talk to her about us... it... the whatever, for the lack of better words, feeling as if a guillotine just waited to make the head of our 'non-thing thing' roll, like it was part of the French Revolution.

"It's like I opened Owen's version of Pandora's Box."

So she is talking about me.

Seeing Ebony's eyes widen when she saw me, I smirked, bringing a finger to my lips, hoping she would get the gist and refrain from announcing my arrival for the time being. Hearing what else Serena had to say could turn out to be interesting. To my surprise, the girl behind the counter just nodded, actually keeping her mouth shut and letting Serena rant on without saying a word. Ebony was Serena's friend/shop manager/girl Friday, and I was sure there should have been some sort of girl code that would make her mention I was within earshot. Maybe, like me, she was too curious to pass up hearing the rest of Serena's side of the story, though.

"I mean, seriously, who the fuck freaks out when someone basically tells them they want them?"

"That sounds sexual," Ebony chuckled. "More like opening pants than boxes."

"Oh, shut it. You know what I mean. When someone tells them they want them in more than one way."

"Still sexual. Now it just sounds like you're trying to say on top of you, underneath you, behind you, in front of you, upside down..."

Upside down?

Suppressing a chuckle and resisting the temptation to ask Ebony if there were any chance I could watch the latter at some point, I sat down on the sofa in the waiting area, all ears, more than happy that I had walked in at the right moment, even if I couldn't be sure I would end up liking what I was about to hear. After all, Serena didn't seem happy with how our conversation had ended, considering she had just referred to me as a 'rawr-rawr-ing' grizzly bear. Personally, I liked being described as a grizzly bear rather than a teddy bear, but that was beside the point.

"Fuck you, Ebbs. I'm trying to figure out if I want to keep things going the way they have been, or if I need to give him an ultimatum, or whatever you want to call it. I just don't want this to somehow fall back on Jaden."

"Who's Jaden?" I asked. *So much for eavesdropping.*

I remembered Serena mentioning someone from her past whom she wanted to turn into her future, but I wasn't exactly sure how us being in a relationship would contribute to her achieving that. Wouldn't it have put a prospective boyfriend off? Unless he was the kind of guy who always wanted what he couldn't have... which sounded a little all too close to home.

"Why the hell didn't you tell me he was here?" Serena hissed at Ebony as she joined us in the front room, flinging a pair of rubber gloves at her friend.

Whoops.

"Figured you heard the door." Ebony shrugged casually, pretending like it hadn't been a big deal she had basically agreed to my request to stay quiet, rather than being loyal to Serena. Truth be told, I wasn't entirely sure which one of us would end up being in trouble over that.

"You could have just been letting in some fresh air. What do I know?" My favorite artist shrugged with a sigh, eyeing me, probably trying to figure out how much I had heard.

"First thing I heard was about me eating you." I smiled sweetly, deciding to add to the unnecessary innuendo. "I really like that shade of lipstick you're wearing, by the way. Know where else that'd look good?"

"If you say on your cock, I'll staple that fucker to your ass cheeks." The sincerity with which those words left Serena's lips made me laugh, despite their content.

Only Serena...

"Must be a pretty impressive size for you to make threats like that," Ebony chimed in, giggling, earning a glare from Serena. *She must be the one in trouble then, not me... I hope.* She seemed to think so, as well, because she quickly added that she was going to grab some coffee and a pack of cigarettes as she picked up her purse and headed out, leaving us unsupervised.

"What was it I said about visits at work, Connors?" Serena asked after a moment of not quite awkward silence, picking up the gloves she had thrown at Ebony.

"Hey. I stayed in the waiting area and didn't say a word this time, just in case you were with a client. I actually behaved for a change, learned a new trick."

"You mean you didn't say shit because you wanted to listen to a conversation that wasn't yours to listen to." The fact that the corners of her lips tugged up ever so slightly took away some of the severity her words could have otherwise had, calming the waters a little... or my pulse, depending on how you looked at it.

"Basically," I admitted, nodding. "So... Any verdict on whether I'm presented with an ultimatum? Or do I get the chance to just keep things going the way they have been?"

"When you put it like that, it isn't hard to see which one you'd rather have, Owen."

"I just don't see the sense in putting a label on this, Serena. I mean, why do we have to? What's wrong with how things have been?"

"Nothing, but I don't think us spending that much time together, being seen out together, when you have a herd of harlots following you around, is going to help my case with Jaden."

"Who's Jaden?" I asked, repeating my former, still unanswered question. She knew why I didn't want a relationship, so it was only fair for her to tell me why she did.

"Remember that thing about keeping things locked up, about not sharing them? Jaden's what's inside my locked box, and I really don't feel like opening it right now. He's... a story for another day, in the not too near future."

"So you have an ulterior motive for a label, but I can't know what it is?" I frowned, unable to connect what may have been right in front of me had I put more effort into connecting the dots, into reading between the lines.

"Yes, and yes. But I also think that this, us, actually does have potential. I like you, Owen. I like us... when we're not discussing something as stupid as giving this a name."

"If the image is what you're concerned about, I haven't been sleeping with anyone else for a while now, Serena, so what you just called a 'herd of harlots' won't be a problem. However, I must say I do like the wording. It'd be a great title for a song."

"You're a dumbass," she chuckled, brushing her hair back.

"Took away the seriousness, though, didn't it?" I shrugged innocently. Simplicity had always been one of my favorite parts about her and me, and we had started to lack that.

"But, Owen, it's important that if you do sleep with someone else, or a lot of someones, it won't come crashing down on me. If it looks like we are in a relationship, I need you to be committed to that, even if just on the outside, because I need to act responsible. Be responsible, to be exact. Which I am, but I also need to look it to an outsider. The thing I don't want to talk about right now? It's more important to me than I could possibly put into words, so…"

"If you need me to be, I'll be the best fake boyfriend anyone could ask for, Serena. I promise. And I know I'm being somewhat of an ass here, but I don't want to be an even bigger one by lying about wanting a label. I don't. Not right now. Maybe at some point, but not yet. Not because I don't like you, I think we both know I do, but because we also both know I'm hopelessly hooked on someone I haven't quite managed to entirely let go of yet."

"We both got baggage, loaded to the max, don't we?"

There was no denying how right she was, so I nodded. "I don't think we'd make it past airport security."

It seemed we had just added part of the other's baggage to our own, too, which felt both nice and frightening at the same time. Maybe we were already more in a relationship than I wanted to admit.

Chapter 19

When I was a teenager, my mother always claimed that time flew, especially when you kept busy with the things you loved, and even more so as you grew older. And I, of course, disagreed repeatedly – not only because, as her son, it was my duty to not agree on a regular basis, but first and foremost because my teenage self had failed to see any logic in it at the time. Time was time, be it a minute or an hour... sixty of one making up one of the other, twenty-four of which would add up to a day.

I had experienced time seemingly passing slower when I was bored out of my mind, but when it actually whooshed by, it was an unknown phenomenon to me.

When the band wasn't doing press or promo, we either hung out or practiced for the upcoming second leg of the tour, sometimes even working on additional new material with me mostly composing lyrics, while we all collaborated on the correlating tunes, as always.

When I wasn't busy with the boys, I had Lyric. Despite no longer having to keep what she and Trent had a secret, she still... or maybe even especially... kept finding new, not entirely uncreative ways to play on my nerves. She was, after all, my sister. What kind of sibling would she be had she not made a nuisance of herself?

And then there was Serena. Serena, who kept me busy when nothing else would, and who – voluntarily, yet probably by accident – kept me from having too much time to sulk. I sometimes felt a bit bad about the casualness of us, even though she had known from the start that she couldn't have my heart because it was held captive by somebody else. However, it had started to feel a little less crushed by the day.

She and I, we both had our baggage full of heartache and things we didn't talk about, which seemed to connect us in strange, yet comforting ways. I didn't talk about Rayven, she didn't talk about Jaden, and we were both perfectly fine with that. We had each other, trying to keep the other sane through whatever storm raged around and, most importantly, inside us.

Time.

Such a funny thing.

"Cut!" the director of our new music video called for what seemed like the hundredth time that day. The location, an old warehouse, was hot and stuffy, probably thanks to the amount of people we had on set trying to make some scenes look like they had been shot at an actual show without having played the songs on stage yet, and time seemed to stand still whenever changes were being discussed.

After a day of repeating some things several times so they could get the "best angles" and the "perfect lighting", not that I cared, I couldn't wait to get out of there. Maybe pouring my heart and soul into the lyrics for our new album hadn't been the best idea, considering things like video shoots required me to listen to the same songs over and over again. It felt as if buckets of salt were continuously being scrubbed into each and every one of my not yet entirely healed emotional scars – or emotional wounds, if you will.

"All right, guys. One more with a different crowd to give us a variety of shots to choose from, then we'll call it a day."

We were instructed to get back on our marks, the guys about to start playing their instruments again, me singing, even though both would be covered by a studio-recorded version of the song later to ensure a clean sound. I suppose the fans who showed up to be in the video had also gotten instructions of when to come in, where to stand, what to do, because they moved to their places, too. It was strange to do a video like that, basically faking a concert, but if people who knew what they were doing said that was how it was done, that was how it was done. I guess it was a great experience for anyone who took the time to be a part of the project because they actually liked our music.

Thankfully, they told us to go through the whole song for the next shot, which would also be the last of the day, rather than doing bits and pieces before resetting and starting all over again. Taking a deep breath, I closed my eyes for a moment, the same as I would have in front of a big audience, before letting the lyrics roll off my tongue.

Where have you been
All these years?
I know you're out there
Somewhere.
Out in the real world.
[Where have you been?]
'Cause I never made an appearance
In a fairy tale.

Pawns in a game,
You and I.
We're made from the same wood,
You and I.
But this is no once upon a time
'Cause I never made an appearance,
An appearance in a fairy tale.

I see your reflection in the shards of glass.
You're the fuckin' Queen of Hearts,
Turned me into the Jester.
I'm all in.
[All in, but you're out.]

Cards on the table.
[All in!]
It seems like just yesterday
I lost the game.
Does it ever end?
The charade to mask the pain?

What's the way out
When there seems to be no elucidation?
[Are you a figment of my hallucination?
Will it ever end?]
The devil, herself, carved our future,
Charcoal black,
Endless Labyrinth.
[Did you get lost?]

Where have you been
All these years?
[Are you lost?]

I know you're out there
Somewhere.
Out in the real world.
[Where have you been?]
Or a pawn on someone else's playing board?
[Are you lost?]
'Cause I never made an appearance
In a fairy tale.
Time's up.
The hourglass has run out.
Charcoal black,
[Pitch black]
Endless labyrinth,
[Time's up]
This is the end.
[No happy end]

I could have sworn I saw the subject of the song, the one who the whole damn album was about, when my eyes wandered to engage with the audience during our performance, but with how much everyone moved around, bodies jumping, lights flashing, cameras being shoved into my face, it had been hard to keep track of one particular person in the sea of people, despite it not being a full-sized concert.

As soon as the track ended, our spectators were ushered outside. I could only hope Rayven, or the girl I had thought to be her, would be waiting outside when we were done. I had a million questions shooting through my mind, my heart pounding, as if it were trying to escape from the false safety created by my ribcage.

Stupid heart.

I ached to get outside, not even waiting for the guys before I stormed off the makeshift stage. Of course, that meant just about everyone was still outside, which lead to me having to pose for a ton of pictures. I didn't usually mind. After all, every single one of them had shown up just for us, taken the time to support us by being in our new video, so it was the least any of us could do in return.

Plastering on a smile, I *almost* patiently took photo after photo, signed CDs, and engaged in short chitchats, my eyes scanning the faces of those around me every chance I got, looking for *her*.

She couldn't just have been a figment of my imagination, could she? She had looked so real, so... *her*, but my hopes crumbled a little with every person who left, decreasing the probability of her still being around... if she had ever been there in the first place.

"Fucking hell, I could have sworn it was her," I grumbled as I returned to the makeshift backstage area, which was separated from the rest by curtains and crates, throwing a plastic bottle full of water into the wall. Everyone hanging out in our little hiding spot was probably happy it wasn't glass, which would have been hazardously sent flying all over the place.

Like those fucking snow globes.

"Aren't you a little old for imaginary friends, twatwaffle?" Jimmy asked, sounding a lot more amused than I felt. While I was fairly certain he hadn't meant for his words to resonate with me in a bad way at all, I could barely keep my fist from meeting his face. Instead, I slapped my hands down on the crate he was sitting on.

"Stop taking the piss, man! I know what I saw!"

"We all know what you *want* to see, Owen. What you think you *may* have seen...," Jake threw in with an almost exasperated sigh.

Thanks for the support, jerk.

"What's that supposed to mean?" I already knew the answer, but it was one I didn't like. The guys didn't believe she'd actually been there. To be fair, her not being outside made me more than just a little doubtful, too, but admitting I had seen her without her actually being there would have made me feel like I had genuinely started losing my mind, losing control. That was something I couldn't accept. It threw me into an emotional downward spiral. Imagine someone getting their first fix of their favorite drug in a long time, then being told it was their very last. That was exactly how I felt that very moment.

Taking a deep breath, I rubbed my hands over my face, still standing right in front of Jimmy. Jake should be glad I wasn't on his side of the room or my knuckles probably would have ended up connecting with his jaw. I knew they only wanted what was best for me, but they failed to see just how deeply Rayven's claws had sunk into my heart, controlling its every beat.

"Why don't you come a little closer?" Jimmy asked, wrapping his legs around my waist and pulling me in, as if we were two lovers in high school. Granted, his unique sense of humor had always worked its charms, usually managing to distract me when I needed it most, but for a change, distraction wasn't what I wanted. Clarity, on the other hand, would have been great, but it was something only I could attain. It wasn't anything anyone could just hand to me.

"I know what I saw, Jimmy. Okay?!" Repeating it didn't make it any better, or any more true, but I still had to try.

"A girl with black hair. Whoop-de-doo. Alert the media," he replied dryly. "There's only a single one of those in the whole wide world, isn't there?"

Sighing, I pulled out of his leggy embrace. "I wish there were some kind of rehab for the broken-hearted. This is turning me to shit..."

"Maybe this was what you needed to realize it's time to let go," Jimmy replied.

"Maybe," I nodded reluctantly, feeling his eyes burn into me.

I had come way too close to punching two of my best friends, just because my mind had played a trick on me. It was time for me to take the next possible exit from Rayventown.

◆

"Well, you dress up nicely." Serena smirked when I stopped by her place on my way home from the shoot. I had been put into a suit for some of the scenes, and after my almost physical fight with the guys, I hadn't bothered to change before leaving, needing a distraction. The kind none of my friends could provide. Well, they could have, theoretically, but I didn't swing that way, and neither did they... as far as I was aware.

I groaned. "Dudette, I can't wait to get out of this..."

Granted, in theory, I had the chance to change before I jumped into my car, but leaving before my mood hit rock bottom had seemed like the best idea – for everyone. Fortunately, the drive helped clear my mind a little, so Serena wouldn't, once again, have to put up with the worst of me.

"No... *I* can't wait to get you out of it." She smirked, her voice all but a purr. She grasped the collar of my shirt and pulled me closer, biting her lip.

"Better yet." I leaned in for a kiss before frowning a little. "However, that would also mean I'd have to get back into it later."

"Are you saying you're turning me down based on not wanting to put that suit back on?" she asked, chuckling, as if I hadn't realized how ridiculous that sounded.

"Yes. No. Fuck it... and me. I'll just drive home in my underwear in the morning," I mumbled against her lips, my hands starting to pull up her shirt. There was no way in hell I was going to pass up on something guaranteed to take my mind off things. Not when it was being served to me on a silver platter. Plus, being with her worked better than any kind of booze ever had, and based on the way I had acted on set, I was sure none of the guys would be too happy about getting wasted with me, even though, despite everything, none of them would have probably turned me down, either. There was no doubt they deserved an award for being the best, and ridiculously understanding, friends of the century.

"Where's your mind right now?" Serena asked, slowly pulling back, searching my eyes.

"In your pants?" I offered half-heartedly, twisting one of her newly styled dreads around my finger. I had never understood the hairstyle. It always reminded me of a dog's matted fur.

"That's... a first," she chuckled, raising her eyebrows at me. *Did I say that last part out loud?* "If you're talking about matted fur, though, I'm not sure whose pants your mind's in because, last time I checked, there wasn't *any* kind of fur in mine."

"Wow." I couldn't help but chuckle, clearing my throat a bit as I ran a hand through my hair. "I can't save that one by saying I was talking about what's on your head, can I?"

"Barely. I mean, it still wouldn't be any nicer, but at the same time, it'd be a little less, uhm, disturbing? You wouldn't wanna be called a flea-sack, either, would you?"

"*So* not the same thing." I shook my head. How had she even come up with that?

"Whatever. Shut up and go back to kissing me."

"Yes, ma'am." I smirked, our lips only meeting briefly. Wanting to say something, I pulled back a bit, her mouth making its way to my neck the moment I had set it free again. "You should come on tour with us."

"What?" she frowned, taking a step back, putting some distance between us.

Shit.

"Tour with us. Just for a few stops... not the whole thing halfway around the world."

"You... want me to... come?" Serena sounded incredulous, the apparently unintended innuendo quickly making her add, "Along, I mean?"

"Distraction to go sounds like the perfect thing to take with me," I offered with a lopsided smirk. Judging by the little huff escaping her, it wasn't the right thing to say, but she shrugged a bit anyway. "Was that a yes? A no? A maybe? I think I may have played hooky the day shrug interpretation was discussed in school."

"It depends."

"On what?" I bit the inside of my cheek a bit, praying her answer wouldn't involve anything even remotely related to labeling.

Baby steps.

"On how well you perform before hitting the road again," she replied with a wicked glint in her eyes.

Her lips crushed back onto mine, bringing an end to verbal communication for the night... unless you counted the few words that could have, with some imagination, been made out in between all the groans and moans echoing throughout her apartment in the hours to follow.

Chapter 20

Serena had decided to join us on the road for a little while, saying she wanted to take a break and travel a little. Knowing we needed someone to take care of the merchandise booth at our shows, who would I have been to turn her down when she asked if the offer to take her along still stood? Plus, it meant some extra fun for me... a lot of it, actually. Dirty deeds between the sheets. Panty-rage backstage. Fucking on the floor after the encore. Blows after bows.

"So...," Serena started as she plopped down on the cushioned bench next to me, swinging her legs over mine.

Our driver maneuvered the bus down one highway or another, inching us closer to our next destination, while Chuck snored so loudly, I feared he might end up attracting some wild moose. There was only one kind of animalistic groupie I liked, and that came in a very human form.

"So what?" I prompted, picking at the fabric of her leggings, letting it snap back to her skin, chuckling when she slapped my hand away.

I would never understand that piece of clothing. Sure, it was tight, and could generally show off some great, and a lot of not so great – all I'm saying is camel toe – features, but how exactly were leggings any different from underwear? Tights were considered underwear, too, weren't they? Leggings were just as clingy, and only a little less see-through.

"Lace panties would be a hell of a lot better," I mumbled, earning another playful slap from Serena. Apparently, she wasn't too enthused by my musings.

"Dude! The view wouldn't be anything new to *you*, but I'm *so* not parading around the bus in my underwear." Underlining her words with a dramatic sigh, she poked my chest. "Where are we off to next?" When I didn't reply, she said, "Next up's Chicago, right?"

My mind was still preoccupied with premature gutter talk, but at least I did it silently for a change. That was sure to be rather refreshing to our fellow travelers, even though they were more than used to it... and were exactly the same.

Chapter 21

I wiped the sweat off my face with the bottom of my shirt as we walked back onto the stage for an encore, the noise erupting from the crowd deafening. As I picked up my guitar and pulled the strap over my shoulder, I threw a quick glance toward the right side of the stage, the adrenaline induced smile stuck in place, making sure Lyric and Serena still stood where they had been just moments ago... right by the stage, in front of the security barriers. Safe and sound.

Wrapping my hands around the microphone, I closed my eyes and took a deep, calming breath as the boys started playing the intro to the upcoming song. "Devil Knows" was one of my favorite songs from our latest album, and one of the two encore songs we had added to the set list, "Make It All Right" being the other one. Joining in with my guitar when the time was right, I let the words flow, the lyrics playing their own little song on my vocal chords.

The devil would know.
You're a raven, not a crow.
I'd search for you in the deepest, darkest labyrinth.
You're my poison, like a bottle of absinthe.
So many deaths to die,
So much 'why, oh why?'
[Why? Why? Why?]
Are you an angel, turned to concrete?
[Show me your halo.]
Where's your heart's beat?
[Say, does it still beat?]

Can't see you.
Can't hear you.
I feel you.

You are the death of me
Emotionally.
You are the light I see,
Like a candle in the wind – uncertainty.

Up to that point, I had kept my eyes closed. It was easier to put true feelings into every word when you weren't distracted by your audience's every movement or blinded by the spotlights bright enough to make a blind man see, figuratively speaking. To better convey what the song was about, though, the stage seemed to be the darkest part of the stadium, so when I opened my eyes, it was the crowd that was illuminated, allowing me to not just see one big sea of people, but actual faces. And that was when I thought I spotted a face I hadn't expected to ever see again.

Put me in a grave.
I am my heart's slave.
I see you in a crowded room.
Meeting you was doom.

Closing my eyes again, I tried to stay focused, convinced I was losing my mind. My eyes had probably betrayed me. Big time. It was the rush, the adrenaline, the lyrics. It must have been.

This ain't a love song.
Hope is all wrong.
I love you,
But I don't want to.
[I never meant to fall in love.]

Heartbreak, heartache,

How much can a person take?
Losing you was my greatest fear,
But, hey, let me be clear.

This ain't a love song.
Hope is all wrong.
I love you,
But I don't want to.
[I never meant to fall in love.]

Surely, it was only the nature of the song – fuck, the whole album, the entire set list – that had made me imagine those eyes staring back at me.

Her eyes.

She wasn't there. She couldn't be.

Were you just a figment of my imagination?
The only distraction now would be sedation.
[Sedate me.]
Tell me, baby, were you real?
Did you ever feel what I feel?

Reluctantly, I slowly opened my eyes again. I really didn't want to, but I also didn't want the audience to feel detached. As soon as everything came back into focus, I scanned the crowd, expecting to find that very same set of green eyes again, hoping my mind hadn't just played an evil trick on me. But I couldn't find her.

I didn't meet her eyes again, didn't even spy the back of a head that could have been hers.

Nothing.

You are the death of me
Emotionally.
You are the light I see,
Like a candle in the wind – uncertainty.

Put me in a grave.
I am my heart's slave.
I see you in a crowded room.
Meeting you... Was it doom?

Had meeting her been doom? Had I really just spotted her in a crowded room, or had I started to hallucinate? Had my mind made me see what I'd wanted to see?

Breathlessly, I once again thanked the audience for coming out to see us, for creating a great atmosphere, and for supporting us. Gulping down half a bottle of water, I put down my guitar before announcing our very last song of the night, grateful that the spotlight was back on the band, making it hard to see anything behind the first couple rows of people.

Maybe it won't be too impossible not to seek her out in the crowd this way.

Willing myself to focus on the music, as well as my breathing, I listened to the guys play the first chords to "Make It All Right", waiting for my cue before blasting out the words.

With your departure, my heart went astray.
No longer can I keep my feelings for you at bay.

Why can't you hear me?
Why aren't you here to see?
Why the hell can't you hear me?
Why the fuck aren't you here to see?

What wouldn't I give
To know you still live.
Even if I can't hold you,
It'd be nice to know, nice to know.
You just spread your wings and flew, flew away.

I just wish that I knew.
Oh baby, where are you?
Come back to me and you will see
How great things with us could be.
Maybe I had some growing up to do,

And I'm sure you did, too.
Maybe someday you'll come back
And turn me into less of a wreck.

Why can't you hear me?
Why aren't you here to see?
Why the hell can't you hear me?
Why the fuck aren't you here to see?

Bring back some light.
[So bright.]
We'll make things all right.

The simplicity of the lyrics, as well as the brevity of the song, made it easy for us to turn the vocals into mostly growling, rather than singing – which was also the reason we had made it the last song on the set list, saving the track most aggressive on the vocal chords until the end.

With my last word, all light was extinguished. We left the stage to the sound of the crowd going nuts, thanking us with the best sound imaginable, besides music. I couldn't imagine any kind of office job that would feel as rewarding, and wondered what gave white-collar workers enough of a rush to show up to work every day. The thundering end of a show was a thrill I wouldn't want to miss.

"That was fuckin' amazing!" Jimmy exclaimed, all but dancing back toward the dressing rooms.

Maybe I should have suggested cute little tutus as our stage outfits – or his anyway. I was sure there were plenty of people out there who would have gone absolutely berserk to see him rock a tutu paired with a leather jacket... a combination Lyric had always made her male Barbie dolls wear, for reasons that were beyond me.

"Dude, what's that look for? You don't agree?" Jimmy asked as his eyes met mine during one of his pirouettes. It was the best way to describe what he was doing.

"No, I... Sorry. I was just... imagining you in a ballet skirt." I chuckled, running a hand through my hair.

"Huh... Your bed bunny's out there, yet you're debating setting sail for the other shore?"

"'Setting sail for the other shore'? Really?"

"It's all in the alliteration. You're not the only one with a way for words, little duckling."

"Your parents let you get away with way too much growing up."

"Someone's gotta be the light in the darkness," he chuckled.

Although it was obvious he was only joking, I couldn't help but think about how right he was. We all needed some kind of guiding light, making sure we got through this mess called life. No matter how good we thought we were doing on our own, things always seemed better if you added another person to the mix. A human lighthouse. *Your* person, *a* person. It didn't matter, as long as you weren't trying to fight your battles all by yourself.

"Hey, L?" I called out to my sister, who was about to disappear into Trent's dressing room.

"Mh, what?" I smiled when I heard her groan as she stopped, sticking her head out of the room. "I thought we'd moved past you trying to tell me no?"

"Where's Serena?" I asked, fully ignoring her provocative little question, which she had surely only asked to make a statement.

Accepting what Trent and she had wasn't easy for me, but as long as they were both happy, I wasn't going to interfere any longer. I knew what being away from the one you loved was like, and I really didn't wish that feeling of endless longing and desperation on anyone. Falling for someone you couldn't have was like falling into a bottomless pit. Dark and lonely, no matter how many people you surrounded yourself with. At one point, even I realized it had started making me somewhat bitter. Cynical.

While Serena and I still weren't even close to "girlfriending", as she had called it in the very beginning of our little arrangement, we had reached a very comfortable stage of "friends with benefits", a status I had no intention of changing. As far as I was aware, neither did she. Not anymore. It was working out pretty well. Between her and the new album, I had enough outlets to not constantly let the memories of Rayven drag me down. It wasn't like she had been forgotten, or that I wasn't still utterly in love with her, but I was positive I had found a better way to cope, one that allowed the people around me to not constantly suffer under my moods.

"Checking out what's left of the merch, like she isn't screwing the vocalist."

"She's probably buying everything and sending it to Mom, who's trying to make sure we have at least one customer." I smirked, rubbing my neck a bit. I was still convinced that, in the beginning, Mom had gone around and paid people to come to our shows, but we had now gotten to a point where that wasn't necessary anymore. The stadium was packed every night, as crowded as we had always hoped our concerts would be.

Put me in a grave.
I am my heart's slave.
I see you in a crowded room.
Meeting you... Was it doom?

"Earth to Ow-Ow?"

Lyric's voice sounded like it came from far away, and it took me a moment to realize I must have zoned out. She had stepped back into the hallway, only standing a few feet from me, regarding me, concern written all over her face. "Are you all right? You look like you've seen a ghost."

"I... I guess I may have," I mumbled, clearing my throat as I tried to sort my thoughts. Had I? She couldn't have been a mirage, right? My imagination hadn't run that wild, not in a long time.

"What do you mean 'you may have'? You had that same look on

your face when you performed one of those last songs. I thought you were about to faint, to forget the words, whatever. Maybe you should eat something. Do you want me to get Serena?"

"Did you just...?" I asked, chuckling a bit, despite everything else running through my mind at that very moment.

"Owen, ew!" With the volume of her voice, she wouldn't have needed a microphone had she been the one performing. "I did *not* ask if you had plans to eat Serena. No. Ew. Gross."

"Believe me, Lyric's not usually opposed to the general idea of it." Trent smirked as he appeared next to her, wincing when she slapped the back of his head.

"Thanks, L. If I'd done it, it wouldn't have been nearly as soft," I grumbled, looking at him. "Unless you want your tongue cut from your throat, don't ever fucking go there again while I'm within earshot."

"Speak of the devil," he retorted, looking past me. Had he not been listening, or had he simply chosen to ignore me?

"Owen?" I turned around when I heard Serena's voice, surprised at how uneasy she sounded. "There's someone here to see you."

As soon as she spoke the words, my gaze was drawn to the tall platinum blonde who had followed her down the hall. Realization, rage, and hope all hit me at the same time as my eyes took in skin so pale and porcelain-like, it would have been hard to forget. Even years after I had seen that woman for the first and only time, I would have recognized that face anywhere.

"Hello, Owen." The woman softly enunciated each word, her

voice sweet, yet cold. "I don't know if you remember me... My name is Chyna. I'm–"

"Rayven's mother," I whispered.

Acknowledgments

To Mom, Dad, and my grandparents – thank you for never telling me that I couldn't, no matter what my next adventurous plans were. When I wanted to learn how to ride a horse, you started to give me rides all over the place, just so I could. When I wanted to learn one instrument after another, you made sure I got to take the classes I wanted. When I wanted to spread my wings and spend a year abroad, you made sure I could. When I wanted to sniff some behind the scenes air, you let me go be an extra, and made sure not to miss my little flicker of screen time, even if you would have rather watched something entirely different. And when I told you I didn't want to just write anymore, but take it a step further and actually publish something, you stood right by my side, supporting me. I know 'thank you' generally is an underused phrase, but never think anything you do – no matter how big or small – goes unnoticed.

Pimpfy and Starfish... I didn't absorb you before any of us were born; you're welcome! Seriously though, thank you for never really ridiculing any of my ideas out loud... now go and grab life by the balls, it's too short to not go after your dreams!

To the dude that put a ring on it... ghost-cherry-ampersand-pacman – that's all! Thank you for the incredible support you have shown me in everything I have wanted to do, for always putting up with me and for going with my crazy ideas. Shoe-airhockey for the win, let's go get some tutus! I love you!

There are SO many people who deserve a thank you – without whom I may have never taken the next step.

Mara - thank you for having been my partner in crime and writing buddy for over ten years! Here's to hoping age will be the only thing changing in the decades to come; non-twin twin - pen, paper, coffee - go! K.E. Taylor – thanks for having kicked my ass on more than one occasion. Don't ever lose that twisted sense of humor! The same goes for the rest of "The Girls"!

Ally Adams – thank you for always having kind words, and for having given me the chance to "work with your boys"! It gave me the courage to go through with publishing!

Lexa – thanks for having taught me English vocabulary that I wouldn't have learned in school. I'm sure you know what I'm talking about!

Kathi – thank you for never having told me to shut up when I was bugging you with pictures of book covers!

Judy – I wouldn't be who I am today, hadn't you and Bob decided to take me in as an exchange student what feels like a lifetime ago and like it was just yesterday at the same time.

David Juteau – you are absolutely amazing. Thank you so much for all you have done to make my cover for what it is. You have taken a leap of faith, and went above and beyond to make sure I had a great photograph to use. Thank you so much for giving Owen Connors a face, and for being as enthusiastic and hard working as you are. Magali from Guiliphoto – the same big, big thank you of course also goes out to you. You, too, have shown a lot of passion for what you do, and without you, this book wouldn't be looking nearly as amazing as it does. Kim – thank you for having put up with my sometimes occurring lack of language skills. I know your job isn't easy – the Queen of the Red Pen you'll always be!

There are SO many people I want to thank, so many emotions to be addressed, but I don't think anyone would appreciate the acknowledgments to be as long as the rest of the novel, would you?!

"Shattered" is the start of an incredible journey – thank you to everyone who has shaped me and my writing, you know who you are!

Last, but definitely not least, a big thank you goes out to each and every one of you who has read this book. It means the world to me to know that someone has taken the time to be a part of my dream. I can't wait to take you all back on the road with the boys in part two!

Thank you, thank you, thank you!

About Becky

Born and raised in a small town in Germany, Becky now makes herself at home wherever she goes. She loves to travel and to explore, to see new places and to meet new people. Becky has been an avid reader and a creator of wor(l)ds for as long as she can remember, never leaving the house without reading material, a pen and paper. She is a coffeeholic, a binge-watcher, a music lover and professional procrastinator.

FOLLOW BECKY STRAHL

Facebook: www.facebook.com/authorbeckystrahl

Instagram: www.instagram.com/beckystrahl.author

Lightning Source UK Ltd.
Milton Keynes UK
UKOW01f1907060218
317468UK00001B/8/P